LONE WOLF

•••••

Reno walked swiftly to the house, turned, and walked around the corner and found Easy standing off to one side and Lee getting a lesson from Lone Wolf on skinning a deer. Lone Wolf looked up but did not speak as Reno came up.

"Lee, get to the bunkhouse. Easy, you go with him."

Lee stared at him with astonishment. "What's wrong, Jim?"

"I'm gonna have a private talk with your friend here."

Lone Wolf put down the knife, and he turned to face Reno. He was as careful as a man could be, for he knew trouble when he saw it, and he saw it in the tense form of Jim Reno. "What's the matter?" he asked quietly.

Reno said, "You're a no-good bum. I thought you'd amount to something if you had a chance, but I see I was wrong. Here your dad's whole ranch is fall-

ing down, and all you can do is run around and play Indian. I think you enjoy it when people talk about you, how you're different and all. And I think you're afraid to make the effort to be half the man your father or brother is."

Perhaps it was because Lone Wolf knew that Reno was right—and that his father was right as well. Everyone had been trying to be gentle and to tell him what to do. All the time he was acutely conscious that he had to make a choice. But Reno's harsh words and blazing anger suddenly shoved him over the edge, and with a wild cry he launched himself at Reno.

GILBERT MORRIS
LONE WOLF

Tyndale House Publishers, Inc.
Wheaton, Illinois

Library of Congress Cataloging-in-Publication Data

Morris, Gilbert.
  Lone Wolf / Gilbert Morris.
    p. cm. — (Reno western saga ; 6)
  ISBN 0-8423-1997-2
  1. Indians of North America—West (U.S.)—Captivities—Fiction.
I. Title.   II. Series: Morris, Gilbert. Reno western saga ; 6.
PS3563.08742L66   1995
813 '.54—dc20   95-7541

Printed in the United States of America

01   00   99   98   97   96   95
9   8   7   6   5   4   3   2

To Sarah and Russell Serfas
If all the people in East Shroudsburg, Pennsylvania,
*   are as fine as you two, it must be a great town.*
You two have been a great encouragement to me
*   in bringing the Jim Reno series to birth.*
*   Thanks for the many encouraging words*
*   that kept me going during the dry times!*

ONE

Summons from an Old Enemy

"Gosh, it looks plumb pretty, don't it, Jim!"

The two riders who had drawn up on the low-lying crest of a foothill gazed down into the mountain-shrouded valley. Sun Ranch spread out before them, and the younger rider drew a deep breath and shook his head. "Always glad to get home again. Aren't you, Jim?"

Jim Reno turned and looked at Lee Morgan. At the age of fifteen, Lee was on the verge of manhood. At five feet ten inches, he was as tall as Reno and would soon be taller. His one hundred and thirty-five pounds were spread over a lean frame, giving promise of strength in the future. As he shoved his hat back, a thatch of cotton-colored hair fell over his forehead, and when he turned to face his companion, he revealed a pair of light blue eyes.

Jim Reno smiled and nodded at the boy. "Sure, Lee. That trip just about wore us all out, horses included. Always good to be back home, I guess."

Lee studied his companion, a question forming in his eyes. Finally he asked, "Do you think we'll stay on here at Sun a long time, Jim?" He spoke quickly and then flushed as he added, "Of course, I'm ready to go anytime you are, but . . ."

Reno eased himself into a fresh position on the saddle to give his tired muscles some relief. He did it also to gain time, understanding that the boy meant more than he said by the words. He had taken Lee in when the boy was homeless, and since then the two of them had been inseparable, wandering from place to place. Reno understood that the boy was getting tired of wandering around. *A young fellow probably needs to stay in one place—make some friends and take root.* Shoving his hat back on his head, he said quietly, "Can't say how long we'll stay. As long as the Reynoldses need us, though. You like it here, don't you, Lee? Me, I'm just fiddle-footed, but you'll have a place here as long as you want. You know how much Mrs. Reynolds thinks of you."

"No!" Lee shook his head, and his lips formed a thin line. "If you go, I go." He forced a smile, adding, "Well, anyhow, we won't be going before supper. Let's go down and see what Deacon's gonna cook for us." He spurred his horse forward, and Reno followed at once. Not for the first time he wondered if he was doing the young man a favor by dragging him on his travels all over the country. As he set the horse easily to a dead lope, he thought, *I got to make some way to find a place for Lee.*

The two rode across the broad strip of cleared land that held the ranch buildings. Lee dismounted with the grace of a natural rider and headed for the bunkhouse. As Jim turned and reined in his horse before the weathered ranch house, he heard the sounds of glad voices greeting the boy. In the year since he and Easy had come to Sun to look for Reno, Lee had made himself a favorite of the ranch hands, pulling his weight in the work and always wanting to learn something new.

He stepped up on the porch and knocked, and when a voice said, "Come in," he moved inside, pulling off his gray hat. The smell of fresh baked bread and hot coffee was in the air, and as the juices stirred within him he realized how hungry he was. "Got anything to feed a lazy saddle tramp?" he called out.

At once, a woman came out of the door that led to the kitchen and said, "Why, Jim, I wasn't looking for you back this soon." She moved toward him, wiping the flour from her hands with her apron. She shook hands with him, saying warmly, "You come in the kitchen right now and let me feed you."

Lillian Reynolds was a pretty woman with delicate features. She had an abundance of auburn hair and warm brown eyes. Although she was forty-five, she was one of those women who kept her figure so that she could have passed as an older sister of her daughter, Ramona. As a matter of fact, they often wore each other's clothes.

"Come in, Jim," she said, and she led the way to the kitchen. "Sit down. I'll pour you some coffee."

Reno sat wearily in the chair, stretching his legs in front of him. He took the coffee eagerly and downed it, burning his tongue as he did so. He then picked up one of the slices of fresh baked bread that she handed him and larded it with thick, yellow butter. All the time he was eating, Lillian was telling him what had gone on at the ranch. Finally she stopped, tucked a lock of hair up under a pin, and smiled ruefully. "I'm getting as talkative as an old woman. Tell me about the trip."

"It was a good trip, Lillian. We got a good price for the cattle." He sat there, slowly letting the weariness seep out of him, and as he spoke, he saw how hungrily she hung on his words.

When he was finished, he looked across at her and said abruptly, "Lillian, you need to get around more."

Lillian Reynolds was not often taken off guard, but she blinked in surprise at his blunt words. "Why, I expect I go as much as most women." But when his dark eyes remained on her, she dropped her own and said, "Well, I do miss Mona." Mona, her daughter, had married a neighbor, Lew Meade, only a short time ago, and now all Lillian had left was her son, Chris, and he was gone most of the time.

A thought came to Jim Reno, and he said, "Well, we're going to that party tonight. You'll get lots of attention there. Be sure and wear your prettiest dress." He grinned, his broad lips turning up at the corners and his eyes crinkling. "Maybe you'll catch a husband there."

But the joke, slight as it was, disturbed her, he saw. She clamped her lips together and shook her head, saying, "I'll never marry, Jim."

"Well, you don't know that, Lillian."

"Yes, I do. When a woman's had a husband like Martin Reynolds, she'd never be satisfied with anyone else."

Reno felt out of his depth. Martin Reynolds had been his commanding officer during the war, a man he respected. When Major Reynolds had died, Reno had taken on the job of bringing the Reynolds family to the only property they had left—Sun Ranch in Wyoming. It had not been easy, for they had had to fight rustlers and the large ranchers. The struggle had been hard on Lillian.

"You miss him a lot, don't you, Lillian?"

She lifted her eyes and said soberly, "Jim, I think I'll never let an hour go by that I don't think of Martin."

Jim admired this woman tremendously, but he did not

know how to handle this situation. "Well," he said as he got to his feet, "I better go wash some of this trail dust off."

He moved to the door, turned around, and smiled at her. What she saw was a man not over five feet ten inches and weighing no more than one hundred and seventy-five pounds. She studied the dark eyes, the raven hair, the wedge-shaped face crowned by a broad forehead, and the trace of a cleft in his chin. He had sleepy eyes shaded by very black brows, and his teeth looked very white in contrast to his olive skin. He had a slight break on a straight nose and a small scar over his right temple.

Lillian thought, *It's nice not to be conceited, but Jim Reno is just dumb. He doesn't know how good-looking he is.* Then she said, "Go get washed up. There will probably be a lot of girls out tonight baiting their hooks for you."

Reno laughed as he left the kitchen. Walking across the yard, he noted automatically the condition of the fences, the stock that was gathered at the watering troughs, the small windmill that operated a shallow pump—all the many details that kept a ranch going. Sun Ranch was a good ranch, but it was still trying to recover from the years when no owner was present. Even now Jim knew it was going to be a struggle to keep it going, though he never said so to Lillian.

As he entered the bunkhouse, he found a typical scene. Deacon Boone, the cook and the oldest rider at fifty, sat with his chair tilted against the wall, reading a Bible. He had been a deacon at one time, and now his faded blue eyes were fixed on the small rider that was facing one wall. He looked up and said, "You better get in here, Jim, before we have a riot."

Ollie Dell, a smallish young man of twenty-two, had hair almost as black as Reno's and sharp blue eyes. He was trim and well built, and when he saw Reno, he said, "Jim, make that varmint get out of the way. He's been a pest all day long."

Patch Meeks, tall and gangly and just under forty, had brown hair and brown eyes and was not noticeable in a crowd. He grinned at Reno and nodded. "That's right. You better do something about Easy if you ever expect to get this crew to that fancy dance tonight."

"Oh, James, don't listen to these fellows. They're just jealous."

The speaker was a very slight young man, not over five foot six. He was bandy-legged but obviously wiry and tough. He was homely as a plowed field, with tow-colored hair and a huge prow of a nose. His ears stuck out from his head, and an engaging smile was on his lips. He was wearing colorful clothes, so bright that they almost hurt Jim's eyes. He wore a yellow shirt, a blood-red handkerchief, and a pair of blue trousers, and even as he spoke, he picked up a high-crowned white hat with a snakeskin band and an eagle feather. He turned and looked into the mirror that was fastened to the wall and admired himself silently. Finally he turned and said, "What do you think, James? Ain't I a sight to behold?"

Reno walked over to his bunk, threw his hat on it, and sat down and began pulling off his boots. A smile creased his lips, and he nodded. "If you drop dead, Easy, we won't have to do a thing to you." He stripped off his shirt and started for the washbasin.

"What's that I smell?" Easy grinned at him, removed his hat, and ran his hand over his head. "That's me. Ain't it lovely?"

"He bought it off a Frenchman, I think," Ollie Dell said in disgust. "Makes this place smell like a saloon—or a dance hall."

"I did not neither get it off of no Frenchman. I bought it in San Antonio, and I've been saving it for just an occasion as this."

Jim grinned and went outside and began washing, enjoying the sound of the crew. It was a small crew, not nearly big enough for the ranch, and he worried about that. They had lost a couple of men during the battle with Slash A last summer, and Pack Ganton had quit as foreman shortly after that. They didn't have the money to hire any more hands, so everyone made do. Finally he went back inside and dressed, putting on a pair of tan trousers, a fawn-colored shirt with a cavalry style, button-down front, and a light blue neckerchief around his neck. As the crew got ready to go, Easy moved close to him and said, "You keep your eye on me, James. I'll show you how to handle women." He rubbed his hands together gleefully and said, "I'm gonna put my rope on Rosie Beauchamp."

Reno blinked and warned him, "You better watch out. Jake Mannings thinks she's his girl."

Easy said, "Well, he'll just have to get educated then. Come on, James. Let's get to this shindig!"

As Jim rode into town, driving the buggy with Lillian and Chris Reynolds beside him, he thought of how many towns he had seen like this. Banning was composed mainly of one wide, main street with a bank at the intersection, a hardware store, a blacksmith's shop, three general merchandise stores, a liberal sprinkling of saloons, and the other small businesses. It was supported by small ranchers, a few nesters, and farmers that lived in the county. Now, as it did on a few occasions, the sleepy town had come alive.

It was the Fourth of July, and Jim turned after looking the street over and said, "Look at those decorations! The ladies have done themselves proud."

Chris Reynolds stirred impatiently on the seat. "Come on, Jim. Let's get down to where the dance is." Chris had recently turned eighteen, and he was a full six feet tall, lean and fit. He'd grown up in the East and at first had resisted coming west. However, once he had gotten there he had adapted better than Reno had ever hoped. He had brown hair, cut rather long, and brown eyes to match. He had the handsome, classic features of his father, Martin, and some of the strength that was in the man. Reno thought, *He was pretty spoiled and rebellious—but he's got good stuff in him. I think he'll manage just fine.*

"Mercy!" Lillian exclaimed. "I've never seen so many people in town."

The street was crowded, and as darkness began to fall, shopkeepers lit lanterns strung along the sides of their establishments, lighting up the street. Reno had to hunt to find a place for the buggy, and finally he said, "There's not going to be room to get everybody in the hall."

"That's all right," Chris said quickly. "They'll be doing some dancing outside. You and Mom go ahead; I'll be along pretty soon."

Lillian took Reno's arm, and the two of them moved along, speaking to friends and neighbors as they entered the large frame building that was used for a multitude of purposes, including that of a courthouse, as well as for the dances. The building was new, but it already was proving to have inadequate space for the town's festivities. Lillian said, "I think Chris must have his eye on some girl, Jim."

"Well, that's what dances are for," Reno said, shrugging.

"Come on, Lillian." He started across the room that was brilliantly lit with lanterns strung from the ceiling. Colored bunting draped the walls, and he moved skillfully through the crowd toward the long table filled with refreshments.

"Jim?"

Reno turned and saw Dave Holly hailing him over. Holly was a muscular man of thirty-two with hazel eyes and fair hair. When Jim and Lillian got close to him, he grinned and said, "Better get some of these refreshments. They won't be here long." He turned and put his hand on the arm of the woman beside him. "Belle, stay away from Jim tonight. You can dance with all the ugly fellows you want to, but stay away from these good-looking young bachelors."

Belle Holly had been Belle Montez until her marriage two months earlier. She was truly beautiful. Shapely, well formed, she had a classic Spanish face, olive complexion, and beautifully shaped eyes and lips. She smiled at Dave, then at once moved over to Reno and said, "I wasn't going to, but now you've made it necessary for me to do it."

Jim grinned and said, "You ought've told her to dance with me every dance, Dave. Then she'd 've been just stubborn enough to stay away from me."

"Come along, Jim." Belle took his arm, and when he turned toward her, they began to move out to the floor. Soon they were sweeping around the room, and Reno smiled at her.

"Even a mail-order bride can find happiness." Belle suddenly laughed, for Jim's face had gone blank. "I caught you that time, didn't I? But now that things have worked out, I can laugh about it." Her eyes went over to Dave and her lips grew tender. "Dave's everything I've ever wanted in a man."

Reno thought about the courtship of the couple—how

Holly had heard of her and written her a letter saying he needed a wife. When she had arrived in Banning, he had seen at once that she was a woman of experience. He had been expecting someone plain, and the beauty of the woman had disturbed him. He had almost lost her because of this but in the end had been able to win her love, and now the two were as happy as any newlyweds.

Jim enjoyed his dance, and as soon as it was over he saw Ramona dancing with her husband, Lew Meade. At once he went over and reached up and tapped Meade on the shoulder. Meade, a tall man, over six feet, with red hair and dark blue eyes, turned at once, and a smile came over his lips. "Well, Jim, glad to see you."

"Don't be too glad. I'm cutting in," Reno said. He smiled at Lew and simply took Ramona in his arms and began dancing with her. Mona laughed, watching her husband's rueful expression, then said, "One of these days you're going to be shot by a jealous husband, Jim Reno."

"A pleasant way to die, I guess. Aside from filling an inside straight, I can't think of a better way for a man to go."

She looked at him carefully and said, "You look tired."

"Lee and I took a herd of cattle up the trail. Just got back in time for this dance." He cocked one eyebrow and said, "Looks like I'm dancing with brides tonight. First Belle and now you." He admired her and nodded. "I'll tell you what I told her: Married life agrees with you."

Mona smiled at him, pride in her eyes. "Lew's the best husband a girl ever had."

Jim laughed, his teeth very white against his olive skin. "Belle would argue about that. That's what she says about Dave." They danced for a while, and he asked, "How's Simon?"

At the reference to her father-in-law, Mona's face grew sober, and she shook her head. "Not well at all, Jim. That bullet wound is giving him trouble. It's gotten infected and just won't seem to heal up."

"Too bad. I hope he gets over it, Mona."

The dance went on for over an hour. Several times Jim noticed Lillian dancing with some of the citizens of the town, including the banker, Dale Devaney. Devaney was a large, rather heavy man—and recently widowed. *Now that wouldn't be a bad match,* Jim observed, then immediately shook his head. *I doubt it, though. Lillian's a pretty strong-minded woman. Devaney couldn't handle her.*

It was at that moment that Dave Holly came up, a grim look on his face. "Did you see who just rode in?"

"No. I've been here all the time. Who is it?"

"Bronte and his bunch." He saw the light flicker in the dark eyes of Reno and nodded. "I'll give him this: He's got nerve enough for anything." He glanced across the room and saw a sleek, dark-haired man of thirty enter. "Everybody in the county knows he's a rustler, but he acts like he's on the board of directors at the bank." Holly's voice was bitter, and he shook his head. "He spoils a room just by coming into it. I'd like to throw him out on his ear!"

"Watch yourself around Bronte," Reno said quickly. "He's no good, and he's dangerous."

Everyone in the room seemed to be aware of the outlaw. He was a colorful, handsome man. There was a boldness about him that many found attractive. He came over, after a time, to the refreshment table, took a glass of punch, then turned to look around. Seeing Reno, he moved closer and said, "Hello, Reno."

"Jack. How are you?"

"All right." Bronte's lips were half-hidden behind a mustache, but his dark eyes revealed the constant care he exercised. He was a man who had lived a dangerous life, and his catlike attention was the reason he hadn't yet been hung from a tree. "You've been gone a spell."

"Took a herd of cattle up north," Reno said easily. He knew exactly what this man was, as did every other person in the room. He had seen men like him before, but none as smooth and subtle as Bronte. He stood there watching the man carefully, and finally Bronte moved away and began dancing with one of the town women.

Everyone was busy watching Bronte, including a man who had just stepped inside the door. Sheriff Lige Benoit was a short, muscular man with black hair and very dark eyes. He wore a simple black suit and a gun on his right hip. He had been sheriff of Banning for several years but was still a mystery man. He kept the town quiet but never spoke of his past. He was well liked and would have made more friends if he had been more open. However he had built a wall around himself that kept people at arm's length. He spoke softly, in danger or out of it, never letting his temper slip out from beneath his steely control.

Now he studied Jack Bronte carefully, a thought gathering in his mind. He waited quietly, then lifted his eyes and saw Lillian Reynolds. For one moment he hesitated, then moved across the room and stood before her. "My dance, isn't it, Mrs. Reynolds?"

Lillian Reynolds turned and was surprised. She had been to several dances, and never once had she seen Lige Benoit on the floor. She was flustered, something unusual for her, but she at once said, "Why, of course, Sheriff."

He led her to the floor, and she quickly discovered that he was a good dancer. He asked, "How are things at the ranch?" And for a while she found herself telling about Sun Ranch, about the cattle, about what Jim and the hands were doing.

Finally, she hesitated then smiled at him. "You're a clever man, Sheriff. You know how to get a person talking."

A slight smile touched Benoit's lips, and he said, "I guess I am clever. If I did the talking, you'd soon find out what a dull fellow I am."

"I don't believe that. Why, I was—"

"Mrs. Reynolds!" The couple turned to see Lee Morgan come in, his eyes big. He almost stuttered when he said, "Chris—it's Chris. He's in trouble."

At once Lillian said, "What is it, Lee?"

"It's one of Bronte's men. He's beatin' him up. Sheriff, you gotta do something!" Benoit at once turned and moved toward the door, Lillian right after him. As soon as he stepped outside, he turned and said, "You better wait here, Lillian. I'll take care of it." He shoved his way through the crowd that had gathered around a wooden dance floor that had been built in front of the auditorium. As at all fights, a semicircle had formed, and to Benoit it seemed the men were like wolves surrounding a helpless foal. There was that cruelty in most men, Benoit knew. The same men he saw from day to day, running their business, raising their families, kindly men for the most part, seemed to smell a fight. As fast as he moved, he did not have time to get there before Jim Reno.

Reno had been walking outside and had seen Chris, who was dancing with a plump, pretty young girl. He had leaned up against the wall of the building and watched as the dancers moved around, thinking what a fine fellow Chris was, how his father would have been proud of him, when suddenly a thick-set, burly man came out of the crowd. He was a man Reno knew slightly—Burl DeQuincy. He had brown hair and a mustache and still had a gun at his side despite the town ordinance. At once Jim spotted the trouble. Chris was too young to the West to be able to know how such things happened, but Reno knew and moved forward, ready to help when Chris needed it.

DeQuincy had been turned down by several of the young women of the town, and his eyes were bright with drink and anger. He grabbed the arm of the young woman, Patsy Claymore, and said brashly, "I'm dancing with you, missy."

Chris was taken off guard, but his face flushed with anger. He slapped at DeQuincy's arm, saying, "Keep your hands—"

But he had no time to say more, for without warning DeQuincy swung and caught Chris a high blow on the cheekbone, which drove the young man to the ground. Chris scrambled to his feet and rushed at DeQuincy. He threw a few wild blows that the larger man blocked easily before throwing another punch that sent Chris sprawling again. DeQuincy raised his foot to kick the boy, and all of a sudden he was struck by a solid object right on the back of his neck. It was the forearm of Jim Reno, who had uncoiled and hit the man with pile-driving force. It would have broken the neck of a less thickly built individual, but DeQuincy simply collapsed. He had just fallen, however, when another man stepped out. He was very tall, no more than thirty-five, and he wore a gun at his left side. His voice was harsh as he said, "You don't get by with that—go get a gun!"

By this time Sheriff Lige Benoit had shoved his way through the crowd. He moved at once, putting himself between Reno and the gunman. Silence fell over the crowd. The gunman saw the star on Benoit's chest but only smiled. "Better stay out of this, Sheriff. It's a private fight."

Still the crowd waited, and Benoit said nothing. The silence spread out until it was absolutely still, and the tall gunman said, "We're not going to be run over by these townspeople, Sheriff. You might as well get that straight."

Jack Bronte appeared on the edge of the crowd and said, "Careful, Sheriff. That's Faye O'Dell. He works for me, but I can't do much with him."

A mutter ran through the crowd, for Faye O'Dell was a man of reputation. He had been a gunman in the Lincoln County wars and had served time for a robbery in which a murder was involved. Somehow he had gotten out and ever since had floated around, using his gun as his means of livelihood.

O'Dell grinned, enjoying the attention. He said, "Better move aside, Sheriff, and let that fellow get a gun if he's got one."

Now Lige Benoit said mildly, "I'll have your gun, O'Dell. Yours too, Bronte."

"No man takes my gun," O'Dell snapped instantly.

"Have it your own way. Give it to me or use it."

The challenge brought a ruddy flush to Faye O'Dell's cheeks, and he said, "Well, I'll just—"

"That's enough, Faye." Bronte stepped forward, unstrapped his gun belt, and handed it to the Sheriff. "Give him your gun." He saw resistance forming on the gunman's face and said, "Do what I tell you, Faye."

Slowly Faye O'Dell unbuckled his gun belt and handed it

to the sheriff. Lige said quietly, "You can pick 'em up at my office when you get ready to leave town. The next time you break the city ordinance, you'll go to jail. You understand that, Bronte?"

"Sure, Sheriff." Bronte's smile was smooth, and he spread his hands wide. "I just forgot, I guess. But if you'll give us those guns back, we'll just be going now."

Lige Benoit handed the guns back. The two men strapped them on, and Bronte, with a peculiar smile at Reno, said, "See you later, Jim."

O'Dell glared at the sheriff, his intentions bright in his eyes. "I'll see you later, too, Sheriff," he said. The two men mounted and rode out of town.

As soon as they were gone, Benoit said, "All right, everybody, go back to the dance. The fun's over." He turned then and said, "Are you all right, Chris?"

Chris nodded, still dazed by the suddenness of the action. "I didn't expect anything to happen that quick."

Benoit smiled and said, "Better go wash your face, I guess." He turned to Lillian and said, "Sorry this had to happen."

Lillian looked at him nervously and said, "I'm glad you were here, Lige. Thank you so much."

The crowd began to mill around, talking about the fight, and Reno was intercepted by Lew Meade, who put a hand on his arm.

"You got a minute, Jim?"

"Sure. What is it, Lew?"

Lew said, "Come over here" and drew Jim over to a relatively quiet spot. He looked at Reno and said, somewhat embarrassed, "I've got something to ask you. May sound a little funny."

"Go ahead. Ask it, Lew." He liked the young man and felt that Mona had put herself in good hands. He was, however, surprised at Lew's next words. "Dad wants to see you. Will you ride over to the Slash A pretty soon?"

It was a strange request, for Lew Meade's father, Simon Meade, had been the biggest rancher in the region, and it had been Reno who had led the small ranchers in a revolt that had broken the power of the Slash A. Simon Meade had taken a bullet at the end of the conflict and had never fully recovered from it.

Reno said slowly, "Sure. You know what it's about, Lew?"

"I'll let Dad tell you. Come over pretty soon, will you?"

"All right. I'll be there tomorrow."

Reno entered the dance hall again, where the music was starting up, and took his place against the wall, wondering what Simon Meade could want. No answers came, and finally he shrugged it off and went to dance with Belle Holly again.

Two
A Matter of Conscience

A buttermilk dawn colored the sky as Reno mounted his horse and rode away from Sun Ranch. He could have waited an hour for breakfast, but he had wondered about the message that Lew Meade had given him. As he kept the big, black stallion at a steady pace, he thought, *Meade has to be pretty hard up to send for me. I've always thought he blamed the breakup of Slash A on my meddling.* He thought of his coming to the valley and how Meade had been a giant among pygmies. There were many small ranchers in the valley, but Slash A had dominated them all. It had been Reno who had stood up to him and broken the power the huge ranch had over the other ranches. Since the time Meade had been shot down in the street, struck by a bullet meant for his son, Jim had not seen the rancher except for one visit. Reno had gone over to see Mona and her new husband, Lew, and had encountered Meade only briefly as the big man sat in a wheelchair. Meade had been obviously very weak and sick and had said little during that visit.

As he rode, Reno looked up at the pale disk of the sun

and said, "Well, Duke, this is gonna be a hot one. Maybe Mona will offer us some lemonade."

The range he passed over as he approached Slash A was good range. It was owned by Simon Meade, but only a portion was legally his; the rest was open graze. As the ranch house came into sight he thought, *One of these days there won't be any open graze.* He lifted his eyes along the endless plains, picturing fences—and the thought disturbed him. Shaking his head, he spurred Duke into a faster gallop, thinking, *Well, it's been good. I've seen it when it was untouched and unfenced, but it won't stay that way long.*

He rode up to the main building and was greeted at once by Mona, who had come out to say cheerfully, "Get down, Jim. It's good to see you."

Stepping out of the saddle, he tied Duke to the hitching post and walked inside, listening as Mona spoke happily. She was proud of the house, which she had transformed by mighty effort from a rough bachelor's dwelling to a fine-looking home. Simon Meade had built it for his wife many years ago, but after she died, it had gone the way of all houses cared for by men, becoming dirty and having none of the more delicate touches a woman can bring.

Sitting down at the chair she indicated, Jim gave her an approving glance. "You've made a right smart place out of this, Mona."

Mona Reynolds flushed at the praise and shook her head. "Oh, it was a nice place to begin with, well-built and sturdy. And I think Simon's wife had it fixed up something like this before she died."

Taking the cup of coffee she handed him, Jim sipped it. It bit at his tongue, strong and bitter, and he handled it carefully, looking down at it for a moment. Then he lifted his dark eyes to her and asked, "Mona, do you have any idea what Simon wants to see me about?"

"No. He didn't tell me, and he didn't tell Lew either." She sipped at her own coffee and shook her head. "It's so sad, Jim. I hated him so much when we first came here. But after Lew and I married, I've got to know him. He's a ruined man, really."

"How's he doing physically?"

"Oh, maybe a little better, but not much. He gets around in a wheelchair now, but he's so weak he can't walk without falling. I'm worried about him, and so is Lew." She was an attractive girl and had transplanted from the East to the West in a marvelous fashion after an initial phase of rebellion. Having never known anything but wealth and the easy life in the East, she was well on the way to becoming a Western woman—though she still made some mistakes.

"I can't imagine what he wants," Jim mused. After a few moments of thought, he said, "Mona, I'm a little worried about your mother. She's lonesome without you."

"I know. I'm going to ask her to come over and spend a week with me. I miss her, too."

"Did you know she told me she'd never be married again," Reno said. He shook his head, adding, "She's really a young woman, Mona. She's got a lot of living ahead of her. I wish she would find a man." The two sat there talking about Lillian Reynolds, and finally Mona got up and said, "I'll go bring Simon out. I took him his breakfast a while ago, and he ought to be through now."

Mona left the room, and Reno continued to sip the black coffee. He looked around at the trophies of the mounted heads, beasts that Simon had killed, that lined the walls—magnificent racks of antlers from a white-tailed deer, an elk, and a moose that had been shot on a hunting trip to Grand Teton. Soon he heard the creak of wheels and stood up as Mona wheeled Simon Meade into the room. Jim kept his face impassive, not allowing his shock to show. Simon Meade looked like a dead man—his face was pale, and he had lost so much weight that the flesh sagged. He had always been big and strong, and now looking at him Jim felt pity for him, seeing what he'd become. He kept his face calm, saying, "Hello, Simon. Just dropped in to bum some coffee and maybe a little breakfast off this woman here. She's not much of a cook, but a man on the grub line has to do the best he can."

"Oh, you!" Mona said. "You never turned down anything I ever cooked. You two sit here, and I'll go cook breakfast for Jim."

After Mona left, Meade said, "Sit down, Reno." He waited until Jim took his seat, and he hesitated briefly. He was a proud man. He had fought his way through life, burying his rustlers, killing his Indians, and fighting off droughts, floods, and storms to build the empire that Slash A had become. He was not accustomed to asking for favors, and he would have done anything in his power to keep from doing so. But now there was an importunate quality in his voice as he said, "Reno, I'm not one to beat around the bush. You see what I've become." He raised his hand as Reno started to comment, shook his massive head, and added, "I'm down pretty low. I don't know if I'll ever get out of this wheelchair. Mona says I will, and Lew, but the doc isn't so sure."

"Well, I hope you will, Simon," Jim said quickly. "You've got a lot of years ahead of you, and the ranch needs you." He added, "But I've been surprised at Lew. He's proved himself to be your son."

A flash of pride came into the eyes of the older man. He had not been on good terms with his son Lew for years, having overridden him and, in his overbearing fashion, put him down. He nodded, and his lips curled upward into a slight smile. "A man has to get helpless, have his back broken, before he realizes how to treat a son. It's a shame it has to be that way."

He went on talking about Lew, pointing out with pride how he had kept the ranch going, and then he said, "But he's got his hands full, Reno."

Reno gave him a sudden, sharp glance. "You mean the rustling that's going on in the valley?"

"Yes. It's worse than it ever was." He shifted in the wheelchair uneasily, reached up, and brushed his hand across his face. "I thought we broke up that gang, but Bronte's got another bunch up in the pocket. They're stripping every rancher I know, even the smaller ones. Of course, they're taking chunks out of the big ranchers."

Reno nodded briefly. "Bronte wouldn't leave. He's found a good thing here, and something will have to be done about him. How many are you losing?"

"Lew says it's hard to tell. They're operating pretty smart. They sneak in now instead of trying to run off big bunches. They'll send in three or four men and get a dozen or so head. They can hurry them along quickly, and we won't even know they're gone for weeks. If it were a big herd, we might be able to watch it more carefully. But if they keep on," he said, "they'll strip Slash A to the bone." He struggled briefly, and his eyes fired with a flash of anger. "If I could just get out of this chair! . . ."

"You will," Jim said quickly. "Don't worry, Lew can handle it. He may have to hire a few more hands."

Simon Meade gave him a quick look and then shrugged

his shrunken shoulders. "I'm glad you're around, Reno. Can I call you Jim?"

"Why, sure. Feel free."

"Well, I saw how you worked, even though it was against me." Meade thought of the range war when Jim Reno had out-fought the huge crew he had. "I hold no hard feelings because you were right. It's brought me a son, but I don't know how long I'll last. The doctor says this bullet wound could go bad any time, and there's something I've got to do before I die."

"Anything I can do, just ask it."

Meade stared at him. "Well, that's a kind thought, Jim, after all the trouble I caused you, and I'll not hold you to it. Most people," he said slowly, "are quick to help when there's trouble. When somebody's house burns down, everybody wants to run over and put up a new house. I've seen men that wouldn't speak to each other for years go to a new cabin raisin' over a neighbor that got burned out. They wouldn't help each other, but they'd band together to help somebody else. So I know you mean it when you say you want to help, but you haven't heard what I've got to ask yet."

Jim leaned forward, his dark hair falling over his fore-head. There was a strength that flowed out of him, even when he was at rest. The rounded muscles of his arms and his chest showed clearly through the thin shirt he wore. He could, Meade knew, turn from a lazy, somnambulist into a ball of fire. "All right, Jim. I'm gonna take you at your word. I've got nobody else to ask."

"Well, let me hear it, Simon."

"I don't know if you know, but I had another son once."

"Lew told me a little about it."

"He was just two years younger than Lew. I was just getting started, a young man, and I came out west to build this ranch out of nothing. You probably can guess, it was tough going. There were rustlers out here tough enough to give any man trouble, and the Indians were far more aggressive than they are now in this part of the country." He picked at the coverlet that covered his thin legs, looked up, and said, "As it happened, my wife took the boy and started on a trip back east to visit her people, but they never made it." His eyes showed the pain that was inside, and his mouth drew into a thin line. "They were attacked by Indians and didn't have a chance."

"That's tough. No man knows what that's like, Simon, unless he goes through it."

"In that, I guess you're right," he said. "It took me years before I could even speak her name or the boy's. His name was Jason. He'd be twenty-two right now, today, and there hasn't been a day since then that I didn't think about him and about Ada. She was a fine woman. If she'd lived, I would have been a different sort of man." He paused, and Reno made no sound, knowing that this subject was giving the big man difficulty. Finally, Meade reached into his pocket and pulled out a folded slip of paper. "I got a letter four days ago from an old friend that used to work on the ranch. He's moved south of here and travels around a lot. I want you to read the letter." He handed the slip of paper to Reno, who opened it and read the following:

Dear Simon,

You'll be surprised to hear from me. I regret we've not been able to visit much during these recent years. I've thought about you often and remember with pleasure the days we had together. Those days are gone now, and we're getting older, but I still think of you often.

Something happened last month that I think you ought to know about. It may be nothing, or it may mean a lot. I'll have to let you be the judge. I was traveling on a trading mission to the Indians and got to know a group of the Hunkpapa Sioux pretty well. They're a clannish bunch, even within their own people, and they stay alone most of the time. Like all Indians they travel around, living on what's left of the buffalo, and they're not friendly. Their chief is named Red Owl. I did him a favor some time ago, so I'm the only white man they'll have come into their camp to bring trading goods.

So here it is, Simon. I was making my trip with a bunch of trading goods, to pick up furs, and while I was there this time I saw something I never expected. It was a young man. At first I thought he was an Indian; he was burned almost copper by the sun. But then I saw his hair wasn't black. It was dark, but there was red in it. No Indian ever had red hair like that. I asked about him, and Red Owl told me he was an adopted Sioux. He'd been taken in a raid. Just as we were talking, the young man came up, and he was naked to the waist. He was pretty sunburned on his chest, but I got quite a shock when I saw a birthmark on his chest, high up just over his heart. It was a dark brown mark, very large, about the size of your hand, and Simon—it was shaped like a three-leafed clover.

I questioned the chief closely, and as far as I can figure out the boy's parents, at least his mother, was killed in the raid, but they took the boy to be a slave, but he was such a fine one, Red Owl took him into the tribe, going through all the ceremonies.

So there it is, Simon. I remembered back, and it came to me that your boy had that same kind of birthmark. I can't say it's your son, but he's the right age, and he was taken at the right time, and he's got that birthmark on his chest. If you want to look into it, get in touch with me at Fort Abraham Lincoln. I'm in and out of there all the time.

A fond farewell from your old friend, Al Denning.

Reno lifted his eyes and asked urgently, "You think this could be your boy?"

"I-I don't know. Jason had that birthmark, all right, and the timing's right. They never did find his body." He put his hands together, squeezing them, and then looked up, pain and hope mixed in his eyes. "I can't go myself, and Lew can't leave the ranch. Neither of us would be much good with Indians, anyhow." He hesitated, then said, "I heard you spent some time with Indians."

"Yes, with the Sioux," Reno said. "As a matter of fact, I met Red Owl one time. Just a meeting—I doubt he'd remember me."

Simon Meade hesitated, bit his lip, then said, "I guess you know what the favor is now, Jim."

Reno looked at him and understood. "You want me to go see if this is your son?"

"Yes."

"I could do that. I'd hate to leave the ranch and Lillian, but—"

"I can arrange to hire another hand or two to take up the slack at Sun, Jim. And this rustler business, it's not going away. It'll be here when you get back. But if this is my son, I'd give my life to have him back."

Reno thought rapidly, his mind running over the difficulties that might lie ahead. He already saw, looming in the future, one difficulty that Simon might not have even considered. "You know, Simon," he said, "when someone gets raised by the Indians, they take on Indian ways, even begin to think like an Indian. You understand that this man, even if he is your son, has been raised a Sioux. I don't know if you know what that means."

Meade looked at him, and a grim look settled in his face. "I know a little about that. But still, he's got to have his chance to know his people—at least he's got to be told about me. A man's got a right to know who his father is." He dropped his voice and said, "And a father's got a right to know his son." The silence ran on for some time, the clock ticking away. The coffee had gone cold in the cup in Reno's hands, and he set it down on the table. It was not something he cared to do, but at the same time, he knew that he was the only hope that the Meades had. So finally he said, "I'll see what I can do."

Meade's head flew up, and his eyes were bright for the first time. "Jim," he said, "if you'd do this for me—"

Holding up his hand, Reno said, "Not promising a thing, Simon. A hundred things could happen. They might shoot me for even coming into the camp, or the boy might not want to come home. If he doesn't, I can't make him come, you understand that?"

"I know. But just to know that you're going, Jim—that means a lot to me." Meade held out his bony hand, and there was surprising strength in it as it closed around Reno's. "God bless you, Reno." He held onto the hand and laughed with an embarrassed sound. "That sounds funny coming from me. I haven't been a churchgoing man, but I see now that I was wrong about that as I was about so many other things. But, not too late, is it?"

Reno gave the hand a squeeze and nodded. "Not too late." He got to his feet as Mona entered the room and said, "Come along and get some breakfast."

Reno ate a meal and then took his leave of Simon, saying, "You'd better tell Lew and Mona what's going on. I'll go back and tell Lee that I'll have to be out of pocket for a while."

"Why are you doing this, Jim? No, I don't need to ask that. You're just that kind of man."

Reno looked at him, and a smile pulled the corners of his lips up. "I might want someone to do it for me sometime, Simon. I probably won't write, but I'll get back as soon as I can."

He left the ranch, rode back to Sun quickly, and a few moments after his return was telling Lillian about it all. "I'll have to be gone for some time. Maybe a month. No telling how long it'll take me to catch up with those Indians. They wander around like a bunch of birds. It's like trying to pin a phantom down."

Lillian's eyes were worried, and she said, "I'll pray for you, Jim. And for Simon, too." She seemed defenseless, and there was no way she could conceal this from him. Finally, she put a better face on it and said quickly, "You do what you have to do, Jim. We'll take care of the place till you get back."

Reno nodded, put his hand on her shoulder, and said, "Chris is growing up, he can handle things. And Meade is going to send a couple of hands over. I hate to leave you alone like this, Lillian, but—"

"I know. People are always asking things of strong men, and those with consciences just can't say no. Martin was the same way. It was this quality he saw in you, Jim. He told me about it many times. You're a man of conscience."

"I guess so, and I've got the scars to prove it." Reno grinned wryly, then he put on his hat and turned and left the room. "I better get ready—it'll be a long trip."

THREE
Fort Abraham Lincoln

Reno felt guilty leaving the ranch, knowing the threat of rustling that hung over it like a pall. Nevertheless, as always, when he began to travel through the open country he became cheerful again. He was basically a man who loved the outdoors, and the confinements of a town sometimes bore down on him with a pressure that made him feel small and insignificant.

He left Banning and the valley behind, heading Duke northeast, knowing that he had a hard ride ahead of him but not caring. All day long he traveled, and the farther he got into the broken country that lay to the north, the freer he felt. "Duke, I wish we could just keep on riding clear till we get to Canada," he murmured to the horse as they paused at a small creek. Duke snuffled in the water, snorted, and then threw his head up and pranced sideways in a lively fashion. Reno laughed, saying, "You like it, too, don't you, boy?"

All day long he traveled, and for a week he kept Duke headed steadfastly northeast. The narrow benchland sometimes rose to high buttes. All this country was a powder gray, fine-grained land with grass and sage toughening it. It was a land now scorched by summer's heat.

Finally he hit what he had been looking for, the Missouri River, crossed to the east bank, and followed it north. It rained that night, and he made a miserable camp. He was wet and unable to start a fire. The wet buffalo chips smoldered without burning, and Duke was hungry for want of good grass. The next day he followed the river into the rising, broken country and at late afternoon arrived at Bismarck.

The town's gray outsheds and slovenly shanties and corrals he passed by, scarcely giving them a glance. There had been rain in Bismarck that had turned the yellow dust gray and slick and had coated the boots of the people who walked the streets.

Reno lifted his hand, shoved his hat back, and asked a man sitting on a wagon, "Where's Fort Abraham Lincoln?"

"Along that road. About four miles to the point you have to ferry across."

Reno nodded and spoke his thanks, then moved down the street, which moved in a dogleg fashion, up and down and around little folds of earth, past an occasional house, past Indians riding head down and indifferent, their bows pointed outward, their shoulders stooped. Twenty minutes later they came to the river, and beyond, on a bluff, Reno could see the fort, its line of houses square and trim and formidable. He waited for the ferry, then led Duke on and waited until a wagon boarded, and then the ferryman shoved off. The river steamer that formed the ferry was once glamorous but now was dilapidated. It shuddered as it beat its way across the brown, churning river and fell five hundred yards downstream till it reached slack water. Then it worked slowly upstream and nosed into the slip. Reno paid his fare, mounted Duke, then rode toward the back edges of barracks, storehouses, officer's quarters, and stables. All these faced a great parade ground running a thousand feet or better in each direction. Reno hailed a corporal coming down the street: "You know where the adjutant's office is?"

"Down there, by the end of the quartermaster building."

Reno moved along the east side of the parade grounds, stepped off his horse and tied him to a hitching rack, then moved down a boardwalk that skirted through headquarters. As he ambled along, he heard the clatter of dishes coming from the mess hall. It was suppertime, and the sun was dropping below the ridge to the west of the fort. He reached the doorway of the adjutant's office, but just at that moment the trumpeter at the guard gate blew the first call.

A tall first lieutenant almost ran into him, clapping on his dress helmet with its plume, thrusting its strap into place. He gave Reno a hard look then nodded. "You'll have to wait till after retreat."

"Sure," Reno said. He stepped outside and watched the five cavalry companies file out from the stables to the parade ground. It brought back old memories of the brief time he had spent in the cavalry during the war, as the shrill voices of the officers came through the air. "Column right, left into line. Company halt." Horsemen rode their briskly trotting horses here and there, yellow mud spattering the horses' legs. One by one the five companies came up to the regimental front and for a moment were still. Each trooper sat at ease in his saddle. The Seventh Cavalry sat in disciplined, impassive form, and Reno examined them—a long double rank of dark, largely mustached faces.

Presently, the adjutant wheeled his horse, trotted it fifty feet forward, and came to a halt before a slim shape on a fine horse. Even at that distance, Reno recognized the commanding officer, George Armstrong Custer. He remembered Custer from the war. He had been made into a major general at the age of twenty-five, but now was a lieutenant colonel.

The flag began to descend, and the band struck up a national air, then Custer's strident voice carried the length and breadth of the parade.

"Pass and review."

The band broke into a march tune, and the regimental front broke like a fan, and then the ceremony was done.

The tall lieutenant came back, his face purple from heat even in the cool of the evening. He stepped inside, pulled his hat off, and hung it on the peg, doing likewise with his saber. Reno had followed him in and stood by the door. "Yes, sir. What can I do for you?"

"I'm looking for a man called Al Denning."

The adjutant nodded. "The Injun trader here. You'll find him down on the north side of the parade ground. Probably got his wagon there."

"Thank you, Lieutenant."

Reno turned and walked out of the adjutant's office, crossed the muddy ground, and found his way to the location the lieutenant had indicated. He saw a wagon, not army issue, tied on a post in front of one of the shacks. He stepped up and knocked on the door.

"Come in."

Reno entered and blinked in the semidarkness in the room, lit only by the feeble light that filtered through two small windows.

"What is it?"

"Name's Reno. I'm looking for Al Denning."

"You found him."

A man had been lying on the bunk. He got up and came over, and Reno got a clear look at him. He was older than Reno had expected, probably past sixty-five. He was a small man, dressed in black trousers held up by bright red suspenders, a gray shirt, and worn boots. He had strangely colored calico eyes, Reno saw, and a catfish mouth.

"I'm Denning. What can I do for you?"

Reno nodded and said, "Simon Meade sent me."

The trader had been tense, but now he relaxed, and his catfish mouth turned upward in a small smile.

"Sit down," he said. "I'll fix us up some grub."

"That'd go all right," Reno said, tossing his hat on a chair. "I've been feeding pretty thin lately."

As Denning cooked supper, he peppered Reno with questions about Simon Meade. He was a sharp individual, able to see through most things. When the meal was on the table, he sat down and said, "Pitch in, Reno."

As the two ate, Reno was conscious that the older man was watching him carefully, and finally Denning stated, "Kind of funny, Meade sending you. From what you tell me, you brought a lot of his trouble on him."

"I guess you might say that's right." Reno took a bite of the tough steak, chewed it thoughtfully, then nodded. "I thought so myself. It was the old story, Denning. The Slash A was the big ranch, and the little ranchers were getting crowded out. So I had a hand in what took place."

"What about Simon? How is he?"

"Not good. He took a bullet a while back, never has

healed properly. Got infected, I think. He's gone down lately." Reno took a swallow of the bitter black coffee and swirled it in the cup in his hands. He looked over, his dark eyes fixed on Denning, and said, "I haven't convinced you Meade sent me, Denning? Here's a letter from Meade."

Denning took the letter, opened it, and pulled a pair of glasses from his pocket. He settled them slowly on his nose, turned the lamp up, and as he read moved his lips slowly. Finally he folded the letter, stuck it in his pocket, removed his glasses, and stashed them in his shirt pocket. "I reckon Simon knows what he's doing. He always did. Always strong willed, Simon Meade. But then that's the only way any man's ever gonna build a ranch out in that country."

"One thing is better," Reno said. "He and his son were on the outs, but now they're back together. The boy's able to handle the ranch."

"Then you're here about the boy, the feller I seen in Red Owl's camp."

"That's it." Reno took another swallow of the coffee and put it down. "I told Simon if the boy's grown, been raised by the Sioux, it's not a matter of just giving him an invitation."

"By George, you got that right!" Denning beat his fists on the table. "Sometimes I wish I hadn't even writ Simon. But there it is—a man's got a right to know if his boy's alive, and the boy's got a right, too, I reckon."

"I guess you're right. I'll have to do what I can."

Denning stared at him, drumming his fingers on the table. "What you wanna do, Reno?"

"Go to Red Owl, talk to the boy, let him make up his own mind."

"You'll raise hob doing that," Denning insisted. His

twisted mouth turned trap-tight, and he shook his head almost violently. "That country they're in—the government done set it apart as an Indian reservation. No white men allowed."

"I didn't know that," Reno said in surprise.

"Well, it won't last long," Denning snapped.

"What do you mean?"

"I mean, we never kept a treaty with the Indians, and we ain't likely to start. Why, the country's full of minerals, and the gold seekers are already there. Sooner or later the Indians will be pushed out." He wiped his mouth with his sleeve and shook his head. "I don't think they'll give this time. That's the last ground that they got that's worth anything. I think they'll fight."

Reno considered the trader and sensed the truth in what he was saying. "That probably is so, but it doesn't change what I've got to do. Can you tell me how to get to Red Owl's camp?"

"I don't reckon." Denning shrugged. "You know a little bit about Indians, Reno?"

"A little. What's the trouble?"

"Well, the trouble is, they keep moving around. I know where Red Owl was last month. They're probably gone by now. Only way to find him is just go looking for him—and them Sioux, they don't take kindly to white men."

Reno shrugged, indicating his mood. "I'll have to do it, Denning."

"Well, you can bunk here tonight. I got an extra place, and tomorrow we'll see."

Reno appreciated the bed. He slept hard that night and woke up at dawn when he heard a frying pan rattling on the stove. He got up, washed, shook his clothes out, and went over to check on Duke, whom he'd left in the corral with the permission of a lieutenant. Finally the two men sat down and ate the biscuits and salt-meat and bread. As they ate, Denning said, "I've been thinking about what you're gonna do, Reno." He chewed a biscuit thoughtfully, then shrugged his head. "I don't see you got much to show going by yourself. But if I was to go with you, that'd make a difference."

Reno instantly said, "It would. I'd appreciate it." He sat there studying the man and asked, "Why are you doing this, Denning?"

"Aw, me and Simon was together a long time. One time he pulled my bacon out of the fire. I was a gone coon, Reno! If it hadn't been for him, I'd 've gone up the flue. So now it's my turn, so we'll see what we can do."

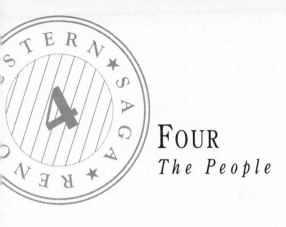

FOUR
The People

Denning was a man who made up his mind quickly, and he proposed that they leave at once. Reno, however, found that Duke had a tender foot and at Denning's insistence, left the big stallion in the care of the army personnel. He insisted on taking a horse with him, although Denning traveled in a wagon. "I've got a mare you can have. She'll be fine in case you have to ride out, which I hope you won't," Denning agreed. They left Fort Abraham Lincoln immediately and traveled hard all day. That afternoon, they camped in a grassy bottom beside the Hart River. There was wood everywhere, and soon they had a fire going to break up the blackness of the night that was beginning to fall. After their meal they stretched out, using their saddles and their blankets as bedding, and watched the fire. Denning began to speak of the problems with the Indians. His voice sounded loud in the silent night air.

"It's dangerous to be ramming around out here, Reno. You know, Indians are all supposed to be inside the treaty land, but some of them wild bucks don't pay no attention to that." He rambled on for a while and said, "What do you know about Custer?"

"Just that he was a general during the Civil War, and he's got some name as an Indian fighter."

"Well, be that like it is, I don't think he's the right man for this command." He lit up his pipe, got it going well, then said, "Back in the war, he won all his battles with cavalry charges. He had one rule: Listen for the guns, then ride to the sound of the guns." He sent a puff of blue smoke upward, then nodded. "That worked pretty well in the war, but it won't never work with these Indians. Especially not these Sioux."

"No, I don't think so," Reno agreed. "They're hard to pin down. All they'd do is fade away behind a tree. You'd be shootin' at nothin'."

"I think a bad time's coming," Denning said. He sat silently, his mouth drawn tight, and said nothing for a long time. Then finally, when the pipe was done, he shook it out and put it back in his pocket. He rose in his blanket and said, "It's gonna be bad out here. I've been an agent for a long time, and it's always the same. We keep pushing the Indians back, promising them they can have the land, and then when we want it, we take it away from them. Pretty soon the Seventh will get the order to take these hills. And when they do, they'll send Custer in." He shook his head morosely and punched up the coat he was using for a pillow. "He won't whip them Sioux as easy as he did the Rebs, you can bet."

For a week the two men moved around, both of them keeping a sharp eye out and their rifles handy. They moved from the Dakota Territory westward into the Montana Territory. They saw smoke many times, a gauzy film that rose slowly in the breathless air of the bluffs—but very rarely any Indians. Three

times they did strike small camps, and each time Denning
tried to obtain information about Red Owl's camp. Two of them
ignored his questions, and one finally shrugged and said,
"Over at the Greasy Grass."

"That's what the Indians call Little Bighorn. I guess we
head that way," Denning said, pointing south. "He may be
lying, but it's the only lead we got. Sounds likely anyway."
They traveled for another two days and finally crossed the Yel-
lowstone River. There was a break in the heat when a shower
fell, but it only made the day hotter afterwards. On the third
day Denning pulled the team up sharply. "Here it comes," he
said. "Keep that rifle handy."

Reno had seen it also. A band of Indians—he counted
seven in all—had emerged from a small stand of trees over to
the south. As they drew closer, he saw that they were all
armed with rifles, and he drew the hammer back on his Spen-
cer. "Recognize any of them, Al?"

"Yeah. This is Red Owl's bunch, all right. I know that pug-
face buck on the right. He's a wild one. Keep your hair on
tight, Jim."

The band circled the wagon, the horses milling around
and some of the braves uttering threatening cries. At once,
Denning held up his hand and began to speak in the Sioux language. Jim understood a little of it. "Hello, Maco. I seek the village of Red Owl."

The Indian called Maco was a squat, muscular Indian with
a pug nose and a mouth like a trap. He carefully weighed Denning's words, and for one moment both Denning and Reno
thought he intended to follow his first impulse and kill them
there. Something, however, came into his eyes at the mention
of Red Owl, and he gave a sharp command to the Indians, who

at once ceased their threatening cries. Maco stared at the two men, then grunted, "Follow." He wheeled his horse and started off to the north.

Denning pulled out a handkerchief with one hand as he spoke the horses into a brisk trot. Wiping his forehead, he said in a voice not quite steady, "Little question in my mind as to how we'd come out of that, Jim."

"Me too. They had us boxed, Al." He gave the older man a slap on the shoulder and a wide grin. "I'm glad you were along. I'm gonna put you back in my will."

Denning gave one of his rare grins, humor showing in his eyes. "Hope I don't collect it, Jim. But the way things look, it's always a possibility."

They followed the band for four hours, and as they approached what seemed to be the camp, Denning said, "This is bad business, Jim. Red Owl's outside the treaty land."

"What'll the army say about that?" Reno inquired. But Denning gave no answer. He only shook his head with a sad expression in his muddy calico eyes.

They pulled up sharply as the Indian camp came into view, and at once Denning said, "Don't make no sudden moves, Jim. They got the best of this argument."

A tall Indian came out, flanked by a group of others of lesser importance, and at once Denning stepped forward and held up his hand. "Red Owl," he said, "I have come to trade with the People."

Red Owl was much taller than the other Sioux. He had heavy shoulders and a massive head. There was a cold look in his obsidian eyes, and he studied the two white men steadily. Finally he looked to the wagon and said, "Come."

"Come on, Jim," Denning said. "I think we're home free."

That evening Denning and Jim sat around the fire with the leading warriors of the tribe. Denning talked too rapidly for Jim to understand much, but later that night when they pulled their blankets out of the wagon and laid them out on the ground, Reno asked, "What do you make of it, Al?"

"Don't know. Big bunch of the braves were out on a hunting party."

He pulled at the blankets, then straightened up morosely. "That's what they call it. But they may be huntin' some Cheyenne. They're a fightin' people. Rather fight than eat. If they can't find a white man to fight, they'll fight each other."

"I didn't see any white man in that bunch."

"No. Out with the raiding party, I guess." Denning crawled into his blankets, put his head down, and took his boots off. When he rolled into his bed, he said, "I don't know, Jim. Sometimes they're gone for weeks on one of these raids."

Reno didn't answer for a while. He sat there looking up at the stars and wondering, as he often did, how many there were. He voiced this question to Al Denning. "I wonder, if a man set out to count those stars up there, Al, how many you think there'd be?"

Denning gave him a startled glance. "Why, I never thought of it." He glanced up to where the black curtain of the sky was literally gleaming with what seemed to be tiny, flashing lights. "It'd be quite a chore," he admitted. He kept his silence for a time, then asked, "You believe God made all them stars?"

"Sure do—and everything else."

"Wish he'd made men as clean as the stars are."

Reno smiled and gave Denning a glance. "As I understand it, Al, God did make men straight. It was Adam and Eve that started us down the road we're on now."

Denning shrugged his thin shoulders restlessly. "I never speculated on things like that."

Reno lay back and looked up. He was silent for a long time, then finally said, "I like to look at the stars. Makes me feel kinda small, but that means if I'm small, somebody's pretty big out there."

"You talkin' about God?"

"Sure."

Al Denning was a hard man and had led a hard life. He had seen some of the signs of hard usage on Jim Reno and knew that he had seen difficult times, too. The reference to God amused Denning. "Wouldn't figure you for a preacher, Jim." He hesitated then said, "No offense."

"None taken, Al." Reno grinned across the fire at his friend. "Just always makes me think somebody made all this, and if he could make it, I don't think he'd make it for nothing. End of sermon. I guess we'd better get some sleep."

As they lay there, Reno became lost in thought. *It's at times like this, out here with nature, that I really think about God. If nothing else can convince someone that God is real, just seeing the bigness of the world and the sky should do it.*

The two men slept lightly that night and for the next three nights. Finally, Denning said to Jim as they bedded down, "I'm pullin' out tomorrow, Jim. These Indians know there's something up. A trader don't stay this long after he's done his tradin'. You'd better come with me."

Reno shook his head and stated flatly, "No, Al. I'll do what I came to do. Just leave me the horse, and you get out."

That was the way it was. Denning mounted the wagon, sat down on the seat, and gave Jim a long look. "Take care of yourself."

"Sure—and thanks, Al. Couldn't of made it without you."

Denning shrugged and spoke to the horses. Reno watched until they were a small speck out on the horizon, then turned back toward the camp. He was met by Chief Red Owl, who had watched the departure of the trader curiously. "You no go with your friend," he said in very broken English.

Reno nodded. "If the great Chief Red Owl will allow me, I would like to stay for another few days. I am very interested in the People."

That was what the Sioux called themselves: simply the People, as if there were no other people, or at least none worthy to be ranked with the Sioux nation. This was common among the Dakota tribes but more prominent among the Sioux, proudest of them all.

Red Owl seemed puzzled, but he was curious about the white man. Reno did not know, but several had already suggested that it would be worthwhile to kill the two men and take their supplies, but Red Owl had quieted this with a single word. Now he stood with Reno and considered the white man. Finally he nodded and started to go.

Reno said in Sioux, which was as poor as the chief's English, "I'll pay for my keep." He saw the chief's eyes light up with amusement and said, "Not with money, but I'll hunt for food."

Red Owl nodded, said, "Good," and turned to go. For the next four days, Reno felt as if he were caught in another world. Time itself meant nothing to the Indians; they lived without a clock. There were things to be done, and when these were accomplished, they rested. Food had to be brought in, and this was the job of the hunters. Reno threw himself into this particular endeavor, knowing that it was all he could do. He achieved some reputation, for he was a good hunter, as good as most of the Indians and better than most white men. One day he went out alone and brought back three deer across his saddle, leading the horse on foot. There was feasting that night in the camp, and the Indians lost some of their reserve. Reno had long ago discovered they were not the stolid people that they presented themselves to be to the white world. When they were alone, they could laugh and joke and play practical jokes on each other. It came as a pleasant shock to him when one of the Indians played a joke on him. He found himself laughing and went to bed with a lighter heart and with less of a need to keep his gun at hand.

It was on the morning following this that Reno, who was washing up in the stream that ran beside the camp, heard excited babbling and talking from the squaws and young people and from the warriors as well. Brushing the water from his face with a bandana, he straightened up, put on his hat, and saw a party of warriors riding rapidly across the plains. Quickly he moved to meet them, still staying in the background.

It was a large party of some twenty warriors, and Reno at once spotted Simon Meade's son Jason. He was tanned almost as coppery with the sun as the others, but he was a white man, as his light blue eyes indicated. The warriors fell off their horses, and Reno could see they had brought back captives and also much spoil. They had made travois, in which they were hauling them, and there were screams of delight from the squaws and cheers of appreciation from the warriors.

Finally, one of the returning band saw Reno, straightened up, and asked a question of Red Owl. Reno stood there listening as Red Owl explained the presence of the stranger. In the conversation that followed, he felt that Red Owl was his deliverer. For obviously the leader of the war party, knowing that Reno had seen the spoil, thought Reno would be dangerous if left alive. However, Red Owl prevailed, and the crisis passed.

For two days Reno made no attempt to speak to the man he'd come to find. He treated him no differently than he would the others; even when he went on one hunt with the Meade youngster and three other warriors, he said nothing of his mission.

Finally, that night he made up his mind to act quickly. *These Indians,* he thought, *are about as stable as gunpowder. I've got to talk to Meade and put the question to him, or my own hair's liable to be lifted.* He found his chance that night, keeping his eye on the party. He had discovered that Meade dwelled alone in a tent. He waited until most had gone to bed. He saw the young warrior get up head toward his tent. Quickly, Reno got to his feet and followed him. His name, he had discovered, was Lone Wolf. He had no chance to speak, for the sharp ears of the young man revealed his presence. Lone Wolf whirled at once, his hand on the knife at his side.

"Lone Wolf," Reno said quickly, holding up both hands, "Can I speak with you?"

Suspicion leaped into the man's face. He was tall, over six feet and well-built, with a large nose and a blunt chin, which Reno recognized as his heritage from Simon Meade.

After a moment's examination, he nodded and stood waiting.

Reno glanced around and saw that no one was near. He began by saying, "I have come to the camp of Chief Red Owl to talk to you, Lone Wolf."

"Why would you talk to me?"

The English was surprisingly good, as Reno already knew. Now, to gain time, he said, "You speak English very well."

"I learned it from my mother. Her name," he said, "was Little Bird with Big Eyes." He hesitated, then added, "She was white woman. My father, Running Bear, took her in a raid."

"Where are they now?"

"Dead."

The bleak, single word and the hardness of the tone told Reno that it was time to speak his mind. "I have come to find you, Lone Wolf." He hesitated, then said, "Your father has sent me."

Lone Wolf was trained not to reveal any emotion, as all Indians learned early. Nevertheless, Reno saw a startled look flash from the light blue eyes. But Lone Wolf said quickly, "My father is dead."

"No. Your real father is Simon Meade. Your name is Jason Meade."

"It is a lie! You have come to search out the camp, to destroy us."

"No. I speak the truth," Reno said. "Will you hear me?" He waited for a sign and finally received a brief nod. Quickly he sketched the story, telling how Meade had not known of his son's capture, thinking that he had died in the raid with his wife. As he spoke, he saw nothing at all in the young man's face. Finally in desperation he said, "Your father is an old man, sick. He needs you, and he sent me to ask that you come back to him."

Lone Wolf—Jason Meade—stared at Reno. A silence fell across the air so that only a faint murmur of voices from those few still remaining beside the campfire came to them. Overhead the stars wheeled, making their fiery points of light. Reno waited, knowing that there was nothing else he could say.

"My father is dead," Lone Wolf said. "I am one with the People!" His voice was like flint, and he turned with a violent gesture, opened the flap of the tent, entered, and shut it. Reno stood there, but there was nothing else to be done. *He'll never leave here,* he thought.

The next two days went by, and twice Reno tried to speak with the young man but each time was rebuffed. Finally he saddled his horse, went to Red Owl, and thanked him for his hospitality. Hesitating, he said, "You are not on treaty land, Chief. You know what will happen if the soldiers find you here."

Red Owl lifted his head proudly. "They cannot frighten me. I am Red Owl."

Reno stared at the tall Indian, shrugged, and thanked him again. Swinging into the saddle, he spoke to the horse, and soon the Indian village vanished behind him.

"Well, a man does what he can. But some things just can't be done!"

FIVE
Cavalry Raid

The shape of Fort Abraham Lincoln imprinted itself on Reno's eyes, and he straightened in the saddle, easing his muscles. The trip back from the Indian camp had been made in a leisurely fashion, and he had been somewhat surprised to discover how much his failure to bring the Meade youngster back had depressed him. He had not known how much he had banked on being able to persuade Jason Meade to return to his family, and as he had sat in front of a campfire at night, listening to the small sounds that broke the silence, he had puzzled over it in his mind. Reno was not a man given to useless speculation, but something about the situation caught at him. He had thought much of Simon Meade, tied to a wheelchair, sick and growing old, and he had seen the pain in the old man's eyes as he had spoken of his lost son. Reno had been around enough Christians in his life to know that part of the Christian belief was that it was necessary to face disappointment with fortitude. He had seen this faith in others and envied it. And now, as he spoke to the horse and proceeded along the trail that led to the fort, he murmured, "I don't know why things come out like they do. Life sure is a mess sometimes."

He clamped his lips together in a tight line, shook his head, and spurred the mare forward. Entering the gates, he nodded at the guards, then crossed the parade ground toward Al Denning's cabin. It was still early in the morning, and he saw that Denning's wagon and his horses were still in the corral. He had deliberately chosen to come the long way around, feeling that he owed Denning some explanation after the risk the old man had taken in getting him to Red Owl's camp. Stepping out of the saddle, he tied the horse. He was met at the door by Denning and at once knew that something was wrong.

"Jim. Glad you got here," Denning said. His eyes were half shut with some sort of strain, and he cocked his head to one side. "You ain't heard about the raid?"

Reno shook his head. "What raid is that, Al?"

"Custer sent a troop out to hit Red Owl's camp." His face grew tense, and there was a nervousness in his movements as he stuck his hands in his pockets and then pulled them out again. "I would 've come out to tell you, but I was afraid I'd miss you on the way."

Reno's mind worked rapidly. "What time did they leave, Al?"

"Late yesterday afternoon. It'll take 'em maybe three or four days to get there, but they got a big bunch, Jim, and they didn't go out to play marbles."

"What stirred Custer up?" Jim asked, taking off his hat and beating it against his side to get rid of the dust. "Something must have happened."

"I don't know. I think mostly Custer just wants to make a name for himself as an Indian fighter. He didn't go with them, though. He sent Benteen in command. He hates Indians even worse than Custer, I think." Denning peered at the single horse silently then asked, "You couldn't get the boy to come, I take it?"

"No. He says he's an Indian and will never be a white man."

"Figured it might be that way. Once these Indians have a captive for a few years, they get mighty ingrained sometimes. Too bad."

Reno stared at Denning then said, "Al, I've got to go give them some warning. Can you let me have a fresh horse? I'll take Duke, and maybe I can outride that column of cavalry."

"Sure, Jim. I got a good stallion. He's a stayer. Come on in and eat, and I'll saddle him up. Your horse is pawing at the ground. He's ready to go."

Reno went inside and ate quickly. He was fresh from his slow ride back to the fort, and when he got outside, he found that Denning had saddled the gray stallion. "You'll have to skin around pretty quick to beat 'em. And then I don't know what you're gonna say. Them Indians don't never believe nothin' a white man says anyway. But I guess you gotta try."

"That's right, Al." Reno reached into his pocket, saying, "I'll pay for the horse and the saddle. I don't know when I'll get back."

Denning shook his head. "No. I'll put this on what I owe Simon. It won't near pay it back, but maybe it'll help some." He put his hand out, and when Reno took it, it was like a vise. "I'd go with you, Jim, but two won't be no better than one on this trip." He hesitated, then nodded, "If you make it, drop me a letter. I'd like to know how it comes out."

"Sure. And thanks for everything, Al." Reno stepped into the saddle, picked up the rope around the stallion's neck, and waved his free hand at Denning. "So long, Al." He put Duke at a fast trot and rode out of the compound, his head filled with plans—none of them very good, he realized with a wry expression on his face. "But I'll do the best I can," he murmured.

The Indian camp was in the same location, Reno saw with relief. He had ridden steadily, changing horses every few hours and pausing once to give them a good rest and feed. Denning had packed the saddlebags with some good grain as well as some food for Reno, and he had made a quick trip. *I should have beat that cavalry. They're pretty slow, staying in formation like that,* he thought. He had already seen scouts from the camp circling around, and he slowly rode in and found Red Owl waiting for him.

"Red Owl," Reno said, holding up his hand under the peace sign, "I must have a talk with you and your chief warriors."

Red Owl's eyes were opaque. He studied the face of Reno stolidly then nodded briefly. "Come," he said. Reno stepped off the horse, tied both horses to a tree, then followed the Indian. Red Owl led him to his tepee, where they had met before, and raised his voice to call out several names. One of them, Reno noted, was Lone Wolf—Jason Meade. The young man stared at him blankly, nothing revealed in his smooth face, and Reno knew that he had said nothing to the others of Reno's offer.

Inside the tent, Reno hesitated. The five Indians, including Red Owl, were watching him cautiously. "I come bringing a warning," Reno said slowly. Not all of the warriors spoke English, so Red Owl interpreted briefly. Reno searched for a way to give his warning and finally said, "Red Owl, you must take your people back to treaty land."

Red Owl's face grew even more harshly etched with pride, and he said, "Red Owl does not fear the pony soldiers. We are the People. Never did we give up our lands."

Carefully Reno said, "There's no time to talk of that. The long hair Custer has sent the pony soldiers. They left three days ago. I rode fast so that I could warn you that they were coming."

Red Owl demanded, "Why would you do this? You are no friend of Red Owl."

That was the weakness in Reno's argument, he had known. The Sioux had known nothing but betrayal and mistreatment from the white people who had invaded their territory, and there was no reason for Red Owl to believe what he said. The hesitation was so obvious that one of the Indians spoke in the Sioux language, saying, "We will not believe this white man. He is a liar like all the rest of them."

Reno made out that much of it and then sat silently as a discussion ensued. He missed most of it and kept his eyes away from Lone Wolf. When he did glance at him, he saw that the young man was staring at him obliquely.

The basic argument, Reno made out, was that Custer had sent Reno to trick them into moving back onto the treaty land, and all of the warriors were opposed to it. Finally Red Owl said, "Enough." Turning to Reno, he said, "We do not believe your warning."

The abruptness of his reply left Reno with no choice. He slowly got to his feet, looked at the Indians in the circle, and shook his head. "Send your scouts out," he said. "They will see the pony soldiers coming," but then he saw that even these words were useless, for Red Owl and the others had made up their minds. He nodded then, turned, and walked back to the horses. Stepping into the saddle, he turned Duke around, led the other animal behind him, and did not look back as he left the Indian camp.

He rode three or four miles, well aware that he was being observed. Finally he was certain that the Indians who had watched his departure had gone back to their camp. He pulled up, sat back in the saddle, and tried desperately to think of a way out. Nothing came to him, and he turned southeast with some vague idea of encountering the troop that had come to raid the camp. But even that, he knew, was useless. Benteen was under orders and would never disobey those orders.

For several hours he drifted across the broken land, thinking hard. Finally he came to a halt at a small grove of trees fed by a brook that wound around through the country in a serpentine fashion. He was hungry after his long ride, so he cooked up his bacon and softened his hardtack in the bacon grease. Denning had included a can of peaches, and, tearing the top off with his pocketknife, Reno drank the juice thirstily, then devoured the soft yellow fruit. "Got to think of something," he said. "I've heard of Benteen. He's a hard man." He remembered one story of that officer in which the killing of women and children had been involved. He could not know for sure that it was the officer's command, but it had happened when he was in charge.

The day drew slowly on, and finally he made a decision. Putting the saddles on the two horses and packing up the bedroll, he tied it down and stepped into the saddle. "Come on, Duke. We'll take a look-see."

He rode in the northwesterly direction, knowing that the truth would come from there. Late that afternoon, he spotted a column coming in a valley that cut its way between two hills. In front of them were flankers, and at once Reno pulled Duke and the stallion back, taking refuge behind a rise of ground. He waited until the column had passed, then began to parallel their journey, staying always far enough away to keep out of sight of the flankers. Exactly what he could do, he had no idea. But he was a stubborn man, and he determined that he would stay until he found something. Somehow there had to be a way to help Jason Meade, and he was determined to find it.

The column stopped late that afternoon and set up camp, and Reno could read Benteen's mind. *Better to rest the men and horses and make the raid early in the morning,* he thought. He made a cold camp without building a fire and was up at dawn after a fitful sleep. He knew that the Indian camp was only two hours away, and he kept parallel with the column as it moved out. When they approached the camp, Reno circled, coming in from the west, which was abutted by a large, sheer cliff. He knew that Benteen would not make the circle this far. *He knows the Indians can't get away this way, so he'll attack on the other three sides.* Tying the horses firmly, he began to approach the camp. He kept on his feet for most of the distance, but when he caught a glimpse of the tepees through the darkness, by the faint gleam of daylight, he got on his stomach and wiggled forward until he was at the edge of the woods that flanked this particular part of the camp. He lay there silently, dreading what was to come and yet powerless to stop it.

It came sooner than he expected. He heard the sound of horses' hooves making a small thunder, and almost at once shots began to ring out. Through the pale twilight he saw that the blue-clad cavalrymen had drawn a circle around the village. On command they began to ride between the tents. Even as Reno watched, Red Owl emerged from his tent, a rifle in his hand, shouting for his braves. But as he shouted a bullet took him and drove him backwards, where he lay still. Getting up, Reno ran toward the camp, keeping low to the ground. He made his way to Lone Wolf's tent, and just as he approached the young man came out. He had a rifle, which he lifted and fired. One of the blue-clad cavalrymen fell to the ground, and Lone Wolf began firing steadily.

But it was useless. The Indians were completely taken off guard and were cut down as they emerged from their tepees. Some of them began to flee, and Reno knew that there was no chance. He moved forward, hoping that none of the calvarymen would see him, for he knew he could not shoot a soldier of the United States Army—he had done too much of that years ago. He had moved within forty feet of Lone Wolf when suddenly the young man gasped, dropped the rifle, and fell to the ground. Reno saw the soldier who had fired the shot lift his revolver for another, but at that very moment a spear from one of the warriors caught him in the side, and he fell to the ground, writhing and screaming in pain.

Reno saw his chance. He ran to Lone Wolf and saw that he had been struck by a bullet that had plowed its way across his skull, leaving a bloody track over his left ear. But he was alive. Reno grabbed his arm, stooped, and with a grunt lifted the young man. He was heavy, but Reno ran as best he could back to the woods. He was gasping for breath when the trees began to close about him. The firing that had earlier been steady was now staccato, and the screams of the Indians were plainly audible.

Reaching the horses, he stopped, pausing for breath, but knew there was no time. With a mighty heave he threw Lone Wolf over the horse facedown, stripped the rope from his saddle, and tied him firmly in that position. Then, leaping on his own horse, Reno moved through the trees toward the cliff. When he reached it, he stirred the horses into a gallop. Finally the muted sound of firing ceased.

"All over," Reno said glumly, and he shook his head in despair.

Hearing a slight sound, Reno turned from where he was sitting on his blanket and saw that Meade was turning his head and moving his legs. Quickly he rose, went over, and knelt beside him. The wound had not been serious; it had only plowed through the flesh on the side of Lone Wolf's head, missing the skull. Reno had cleaned it and put a bandage over it, but it had been enough to render the young man unconscious for a day and a night. Now he saw the eyes flutter and open, and Meade stared at him, confusion in his light blue eyes.

"Take it easy, Lone Wolf. You'll be all right."

The confusion faded, and Lone Wolf recognized Reno. He turned his head quickly and uttered an involuntary grunt as the pain struck him. Reno reached down and pulled him to a sitting position. "You got a crease in your skull," he said. "But you're all right."

Lone Wolf reached up, touched the bandage, and sat there silently. And then he looked at Reno and said slowly, "The pony soldiers, they came just as you said."

Reno shrugged and said, "They did. I wish Red Owl had listened to me."

He found himself being considered by the young man in a strange fashion. At last Lone Wolf said, "You did not lie, then. I did not think you lied, but they would not have listened to me."

He stopped, then asked the question he hated to ask. "What happened to my people?"

Reno dropped his eyes and shook his head. "It was bad, Lone Wolf, real bad."

His brief answer caused the young man's eyes to become half hooded, and he looked around and said, "I will go see."

"That's not a good idea," Reno said. "They may have left some of the pony soldiers there. Maybe they haven't even left yet."

"I will go see my people."

Reno shrugged, asking only that they cook a meal and wait until he was able to sit a horse. Lone Wolf agreed to this, and later in the afternoon the two of them mounted the horses. Reno watched carefully and saw that Lone Wolf seemed to be able to ride, and the two of them made their way back. When they got close to the camp, Reno said, "I wish you wouldn't do this. It's a bad thing."

But he received no answer. Reno dropped back, allowing his companion to go first. There was a sadness in Reno's eyes, for he knew what would be found. And he was not wrong. The troop was gone, and they had left the bodies unburied. Reno never forgot the sight that greeted him as he followed Lone Wolf into the camp. It was like some of the battlefields that he remembered from the war: men in death, reaching upward stiffly with eloquent gestures. There were women as well—and a few children.

Lone Wolf slipped off his horse and moved around the camp, looking down, identifying face after face. Finally he stopped at the body of Red Owl. He stared down at the chief, then turned back to face Reno. "He was a good chief," he said in a hard voice. His face was tense, and Reno could only sus-pect what was going on in his mind and his heart.

Eventually Reno said, "I guess they took the rest of the tribe back to Fort Abraham Lincoln. Do you want to go there and join them?"

Jason stared at him and said briefly, "No." He looked around and said, "I will take care of my people."

Reno knew the Indians feared to leave their dead unburied, believing that their spirits would wander forever, homeless, if that would happen. Reno, understanding the grief and agony that the young man tried unsuccessfully to hide, said quietly, "I'll help you, Lone Wolf."

Quickly, the young man's eyes fastened on him, and there was a long silence. Finally, Lone Wolf nodded and said, "That will be well."

It was two days later before the two rode out from the sight of the massacre. It had taken long to see to the bodies of all of the dead, but Reno had worked alongside Lone Wolf steadily.

That night they sat at the campfire, and Reno cooked supper. Lone Wolf refused to eat, and Reno did not insist. There was a silence that wrapped the young man that Reno did not break that night. He finally rolled in his blankets and went to sleep, half persuaded that the young man would go back to join another tribe. But as they made coffee and breakfast the next morning, to Reno's surprise Jason ate hungrily. He sat there holding the coffee cup, and Reno finally said, "I'm sorry about all this, Lone Wolf." He saw the young man nod, and this for him was a statement of acceptance. Then Reno took a deep breath and said, "This way of life is gone. Your own tribe is gone, but the rest of the tribes are now going to be penned into small reservations. It can never be the same as it was."

Lone Wolf slowly nodded. "You are right," he said. "I have

seen it coming. We have all seen it coming. There is no way to stop the white man." He looked out over the broad plains and shook his head. "It will soon be gone."

Reno said, "This way of life is gone, but you can have another. You have a father who wants you. Go back. Give it a chance. I know it won't be the same, but you'll find friends there, and a family."

There was a long silence, and Reno thought at first he meant to refuse. Finally, Lone Wolf nodded slowly and said in spare tones, "I will go with you."

"Good," Reno said, truly happy that the young man had decided to come with him. "Your father will be very happy to see you . . . , Jason."

Lone Wolf glared at Reno. "I am Lone Wolf! My people may be gone, but I am still one of them. I will always be of the People!"

Six
The Reluctant Prodigal

July produced a furnacelike sun that seemed to burn the grass even as it struggled through the hard earth. Reno and Lone Wolf traveled through the broken country, crossing small rivers that lay at the bottoms of shallow canyons. They sometimes followed the water, sometimes traveling on the narrow benchlands that lay halfway up the sides of canyons. Sometimes they rode along the tops of bluffs, which gave a spectacular view of the countryside. It was a powder gray world with fine green land and sage tufting all of it.

Reno deliberately kept the pace at a slow walk. He wanted time for Jason to think. *Going to be pretty tough on him,* he thought. *Won't hurt to give him a little more time.*

They wound slowly over the countryside, finally passing within sight of a small settlement. Reno had a thought and said lazily, "We're running low on grub, Lone Wolf. Let's go into town and see what we can get."

The two rode into the little town by the name of Brown Springs, and Reno bought a few supplies. He did not miss the glances that were thrown at him as he and Lone Wolf entered the store. He knew it was unusual for a white man and an Indian to be riding together. There was, moreover, a strange look about Lone Wolf, with his light blue eyes and auburn hair. When they had the supplies, Reno said, speaking almost as if it were an afterthought, "Might as well buy you some clothes, I reckon."

Lone Wolf shot a quick look at him, understanding at once that this was part of the transition that would be necessary. "All right," he said, and soon he had picked out a pair of light brown trousers, a tan shirt, and a pair of boots that he could wear. He also found a black low-crowned hat, similar in style to the one Reno wore. They took them all back to the camp, and the next morning when he put them on, grimacing at the tightness of the boots, he stood up and looked at Reno. "Do I pass for a white man?"

"Well, not with that braid," Reno answered.

"I'm keeping the braid." There was a stubborn look in Lone Wolf's eye, and Jim knew better than to push it. He shrugged, and the two of them broke camp and headed on south.

It was a time of silence on the part of both men for the most part. Sometimes they would ride half a day without exchanging a word. But at night, around the campfire, Jim found that the young man was more willing to talk. One night, after they had eaten and were drinking coffee out of tin cups, he said, "Tell me about life with the Sioux."

Reluctantly almost, Lone Wolf began to talk, and as he began to speak, just mentioning names brought pain to his eyes, and Reno knew these were some that they had found dead in the camp. "It was a good life," Meade said finally. "Hard. Not what most white men would want."

"You learned to speak English very well," Reno said. "That's good."

Meade shrugged. "I resisted at first, but my foster mother said we would have to learn to live with the white man. She was a wise woman and said it would be good to speak their language."

"I wonder why nobody saw you before. It's obvious you're not a full-blooded Sioux—not with those blue eyes."

"A lot of the time we were in Canada. We were involved with a raid, and the pony soldiers came and chased us up there. We didn't see many white people. We only came back three years ago."

The fire sputtered and sent blazing sparks upward as Lone Wolf poked it with a stick. Suddenly he looked up and asked, "What is my father like?"

Reno spoke of Simon Meade and of Lew, trying his best to give the young man some idea of his heritage. Finally he said, "You'll like Lew, your brother. He's a fine man, just got married. And you'll like his wife, too." He went on telling about the ranch, speaking of the country, and eventually fell silent.

Lone Wolf had listened intently, taking in Reno's words carefully. There was a thoughtful look in his eyes, and his lips had formed a tight line. Reno had no idea of what was going on inside his mind. Finally Lone Wolf said, "It will never work."

"Don't be too quick to say that."

"It would be as hard for a Sioux to become a white man as it would for a white man to become a Sioux."

"I've even heard of that, and you've seen it yourself," Reno argued. "Some men turn Indian, go live with them, take a squaw, and are adopted into the tribe. And that's after they're grown men, not when they're captured as children."

Lone Wolf looked at him and nodded. "That is true. But, it's harder to join the white man's world."

"This is different. You're not an Indian trying to join a white man's world, Lone Wolf. You're a white man yourself, and the place you're going to isn't strange. They'll be glad to see you."

Lone Wolf sipped the coffee thoughtfully, then shook his head, though he said no more. He was still grieving over the death of his friends and the only family he knew; it would take time for him to be healed. Finally, he lay back on his blanket and closed his eyes, saying nothing else.

Reno, sensing the desolation and fear that lay over the young man, looked up at the stars, as he often did, and finally, after a long silence, said, "Sometimes a man gets thrown off a horse. He's got to decide whether to lie there or else get up and climb back into the saddle. It'll be tough, Lone Wolf," he said, "but you'll make it."

There was no sound from his companion. Reno lay back, closed his eyes, and fell asleep.

The faint light of dawn had just begun to show in the east as Mona put the breakfast she had cooked on the table. Going to the hall, she called out, "Breakfast—come and get it before I throw it out."

She turned and went back, picked up the coffeepot from the stove, and poured two cups of coffee.

When Lew came in, his face was still damp from the hasty wash he had taken. He came to put his arms around her and gave her a squeeze that caused her to cry out, "Lew—, you'll break me in two!"

"You shouldn't smell so nice." Lew Meade had not been a

man to show his affection, at least not seriously. He had not seen that kind of thing in his family life. He'd grown up without a mother and had known only the bleak companionship of his father. Since his marriage, however, he had been somewhat shocked to find out that he could be as foolish as any boy over his bride. He held her now, studying her attractive face, savoring the touch of her body against his, and whispered huskily, "I do love you, Mrs. Meade."

Mona had learned in a short time how to elicit this kind of response from this tall husband of hers. She looked up, thinking again how fine looking he was, with his red hair and his dark blue eyes, how lean and trim he was, and said, "Mrs. Meade is happy to oblige." Reaching up, she pulled his head down, and they clung to each other in a passionate kiss.

"Now that's enough," she said with a slight giggle. "Sit down and eat your breakfast."

Lew grinned at her sheepishly, plopped into a chair, and said with a twinkle in his eyes, "We'll take this matter up later." He began to eat, and Mona joined him. When they were through with the bacon and eggs and he had started in on the doughnuts that she always kept due to his fondness for them, she asked, "Lew, do you think Jim will come back pretty soon?"

"Nobody can say." Lew bit into the doughnut, chewed it thoughtfully, then shook his head. "I think a lot of Jim Reno, but I'm not sure that Jim or anybody else could do what he was asked to do."

"I know," Mona said, "I've been having doubts myself. Maybe it was wrong of Dad to ask him." She had started calling Simon Meade Dad within the last few months, after she had had a chance to get to know him and put the past behind her. This pleased the old man and Lew as well.

They talked for a while, and finally he got up, put on his hat, and headed for the door. Then he turned again and kissed her, saying, "Seems like I'm getting to be the kissingest fellow I ever heard of."

"That's a good habit," Mona said with a smile. Then she noticed as he turned that he picked up his rifle that was propped against the wall. A frown creased her brow, and she asked quickly, "Lew, are you expecting trouble?"

He turned to face her, and his good humor was gone. Scowling, he said, "We lost ten head last night from over in the west pasture."

"Maybe they just wandered off," Mona said.

"No way that could happen." Lew's voice was flat, and he added, "Baldy found the tracks of three riders along with them. We're going to see if we can follow them up into the pocket today."

Mona opened her mouth to protest and then immediately knew that it would be useless. She came over to him, put her hand on his cheek, and whispered, "Be careful!"

He smiled down at her, his good humor restored. "I will. I don't think we'll find anything anyway. They've got ways of shifting those cattle around in small groups. We've tried this before." A gloomy look clouded his fine eyes, and he shook his head. "Dad handed me a good ranch here, and we're gettin' bled to death by these rustlers." He turned, saying, "I'll be back as soon as I can," and left the house.

Mona watched him go, along with three riders, and then she went back to the kitchen. She sat down at the table and sipped at the cold coffee and then got up and began her housework. It was an hour later when she looked up to see Simon Meade wheel himself into the kitchen. He was still able to dress himself and to move himself over to the wheelchair, though it caused him pain.

"Hello, Dad," she said with a smile, and her words caught a quick response from Simon Meade. Her affection had been totally unexpected. He had been without the influence of a woman in his life for so long that he had forgotten what a calming influence one could be. Now as he nodded and wheeled the chair up to the table, he said, "Good morning, Mona."

"Let me make some breakfast for you," she said. Though he protested he was not hungry, she fried another egg over easy, as he liked it, put it on a piece of toast, and brought it over to him. "Now cut that up and eat it, or I'll turn the dogs on you." It was a phrase she had heard him use, and he smiled as he obeyed.

She sat down after refilling the coffee cups, and as he picked at his food she kept the conversation going, though saying nothing important. She knew that he had learned to treasure these times. *I suppose you appreciate the small things in life when you can't get around much.*

Simon said, "This house has been a different place since you came to live in it, Mona. It brings back memories of the time when Ada was alive." He put his fork down, wiped his mouth, then picked up his coffee cup. "You're a lot like her. Oh, I don't mean you look like her. I mean she was like you—cheerful, witty, always joking."

Mona wanted to reach over and put her hand on his arm and comfort him, but she did not. She had made that mistake at first and had discovered that the best way was to jolly the big man along, not to allow him to feed on his old memories. "Well, I'm glad you've learned to put up with my contrary ways," she said. "Nobody else did back East—or if they did, they didn't like it." She quickly cleaned the table and then went to pick up the book that they had been reading together. She had learned that he knew little about books, and he had scoffed at her when she suggested reading a novel. But she had brought one with her—her favorite, *Great Expectations* by Charles Dickens—and to her delight Simon had become caught up in the story. He could have read it himself, of course, but she insisted, "I give it more flavor. You need to hear it, Dad."

She had read to him for about forty-five minutes when both of them heard the sound of horses approaching. "That can't be Lew coming back this soon," Mona remarked. She got up and walked over to the window and looked out.

Simon glanced at her and saw that her body had become rigid. His eyes narrowed, and he waited till she turned around. "It's Jim," she whispered, "and there's a man with him."

Simon Meade's hands clutched spasmodically, turning into fists, and for one moment the room rocked and he thought he was going to pass out. He tried to speak and could not. At once Mona went to him, stood behind his chair, and put her hands on his shoulders, squeezing them. "They'll come into the living room," she said. "Let's go, Dad."

Without waiting for his agreement, she pushed the chair into the long room and wheeled it so that they both faced the door. Her heart was beating fast as she heard the horses pull up in front of the house. There was a silence, and then she heard the sound of steps on the porch and a knock on the door. "Come in," Mona said loudly, seeing that Simon could not speak.

The door opened, and Jim Reno entered; behind him came a taller man. Reno stepped to one side, and the other man came to take up a position slightly behind him.

He had light blue eyes, which seemed even lighter because of the coppery complexion of his skin tanned by the sun. His hair, she saw as he pulled his hat off, was auburn, roughly cut it seemed with a knife, and she saw with a shock that the back of it was in a long braid. His face was square, and he had a determined chin and a bold nose—very much the image of a Meade.

Reno had paused for a moment, and the silence seemed heavy in the room. And then he said, "Simon, I found your son." He then turned and said, "Lone Wolf—this is your father." He took a slight step to one side, as if to allow the two to see each other more clearly.

Simon was looking up into the face of the tall young man and for the life of him could not speak. He knew at once that this was his son, if for no other reason than that his eyes were the same pale blue as his mother's. He had never seen that shade of blue before, not even in Lew's eyes. A tremendous awkwardness came to him, and he said finally in a hoarse whisper, "Jason—," and then he could say no more.

Mona grasped the awkwardness of the situation and said, "Come in, both of you. You look like you've been riding all night. I've got some lemonade. No ice, but at least it's wet."

Jim, realizing her attempts to break through the tense atmosphere, said, "Right! Come along, Lone Wolf. You've probably never had lemonade, have you?"

"No." Lone Wolf had been as speechless as Simon Meade. He had been absolutely silent for the last ten miles, and when he had put his eyes on the man in the wheelchair, his face had been impassive. To cover the awkwardness of the moment, Mona worked quickly, wheeling Simon over beside the couch. Jim nudged Lone Wolf until he, too, approached, looking at the couch as if it were a wild animal, and he lowered himself slowly onto it.

Lone Wolf had faced some difficult and dangerous times, but never had he felt so fenced in as he did at this moment. Everything in him cried out to leave. But still there was a curiosity that kept rising in him. He looked around the room, taking it all in, and then he looked back to the face of the old man in the wheelchair.

By this time Simon had regained some of his poise, and he said quietly, "Has Jim told you about how I thought you were dead, Jason?"

"He has told me."

There was a wariness in the voice of his son, Simon thought at once, but he knew that this was only natural. He said, "I searched for you for years, but nothing ever turned up. If I had known you were still alive, my boy, I would have followed you anywhere." He waited for a response and got only a slight nod.

At that moment Mona came in with the lemonade in tall glasses, and when Lone Wolf took his and looked at it cautiously, then tasted it, he said, "I never knew who my family was."

"That's natural." Simon nodded. "Tell me about yourself, Jason."

Lone Wolf looked around, looked at Jim Reno, who nodded encouragingly, then began to speak. He told briefly how he remembered nothing except being raised by the Sioux and then related how they had fled to Canada to escape the army and remained there for years.

When he finished, Simon said, "I know you've become attached to the people who kept you all these years." Instantly he knew he had said something wrong, although he could not imagine what. He looked at Reno, who shook his head slightly.

"Most of the tribe was killed in a raid by the Seventh Cavalry," Reno said quietly. "It's been a hard time for Lone Wolf—it would be for any of us."

"Oh, I'm so sorry!" Mona exclaimed. When he only shrugged, she added, "But I'm glad that Jim brought you here. We've been so hopeful that he would find you and bring you back."

All three of them looked at the young man who seemed alien there. The white man's clothes that Jim had bought hung on him awkwardly. He had discarded the boots and wore his old moccasins, and the braid down his back was a reminder of what he had been.

Lone Wolf kept his gaze on his father's face. There was no telling what went on in his mind, but finally he said, "I think it is too late. As the young tree is bent, so it will remain. I am too old to become a white man."

Abruptly he rose and walked out of the house, making absolutely no sound as he moved. The door closed behind him, and Reno said quickly, "You'll have to give him time. He's had about the worst jolt a man can have."

"Of course," Simon said quickly. He held out his hand, and Reno advanced to take it. The hand of Simon Meade had once been thick with muscle but now seemed frail. He dropped his eyes for a moment and was like a fallen giant. Reno remembered how strong and tall he had stood when he had first come to the valley only a short time ago. But a bullet had reduced him to a frail, old man. Lifting his eyes, Simon said in a whisper, "Will you two help?"

Mona went over and placed her hand on his shoulder. "Of

course," she said quickly. "He just needs time—but you've got your son back again."

The words caught at Simon, and hope came to his eyes. He said, "Jim, go out and talk to him. If he won't feel comfortable here, let him go to the bunkhouse. Do all you can."

Reno left and found Lone Wolf standing over by the horses. His eyes were back toward the land that he had left, and his mind was there, too. Reno put his hand on the tall man's shoulder, and instantly Lone Wolf pulled away and turned to face him. Reno apologized, "Sorry, Lone Wolf." He hesitated, then added. "Just try it. That's all I ask. That's all anyone asks. You can always ride away—but if you do now, you'll never know what might have happened. Will you stay?"

Lone Wolf looked out toward the hills and the plains that he knew and loved. But he knew with a dull finality that this was all that was left to him. "Yes. I will try," he muttered. Then he repeated, "But as the young tree is bent, so it will remain!"

SEVEN
"Get Out of Here,
Injun!"

As usual, the crew proved to be reluctant volunteers, but Easy gave them no choice about attending services. Lillian had coerced him into going one Sunday back in the spring, and he had found himself walking up the aisle and making his decision to follow Jesus. The new pastor had proven himself sincere, humorous, and full of the Spirit—and Easy couldn't believe no one had presented the gospel so clearly before. Since that day he had taken the responsibility of getting all the hands out of their bunks and into the pews. He rousted them out early Sunday morning with a cheerful "Get out of bed, you heathens! We're all going to meetin'." His words were greeted with groans, and it took some prodding by the feisty little puncher, but finally they all arose and began cleaning themselves for the ordeal.

Ollie Dell looked better than average. He was a hand-some fellow anyway, with black hair and sharp blue eyes, and when he had put on his best clothes, he looked over at Easy and shook his head. "Nobody will pay any attention to the preacher, Easy, or his sermon, not with those clothes you're wearing."

Easy was wearing a brilliant emerald green shirt and a pair of light brown pants stuffed into a pair of snakeskin boots on which jangled silver spurs, and the neckerchief around his neck was a bright yellow. He admired himself in the mirror, nodded with a pleased expression, and said, "You're just jealous, Ollie. Come on, you fellers, let's get going."

Chris came out of the house along with Reno, who had had breakfast with the family, and they stood at the buggy, waiting for Lillian. Chris remarked, "I think Mother's gonna be late for the resurrection." He groaned and shifted around for a while and said, "I've never known her to be on time for anything." At that moment Lillian Reynolds stepped out of the door, and Chris smiled. "Of course she may be late, but she's worth waiting for."

Lillian flushed slightly at his praise. She retained, at forty-five, much of her early beauty. She had auburn hair and brown eyes, and her complexion was flawless, though it took some effort to keep it so under the blazing Wyoming sun. She looked over to where the crew was getting into their saddles and said, "I see Easy's been doing his evangelistic work."

Reno grinned. "Yep. If they don't respond to a cordial invitation, he bends his gun over their head—or threatens to." He turned to look at the woman beside him. "You look beautiful, Lillian."

"Why, thank you, Jim." She stepped down from the porch, and Reno handed her into the buggy then went around to get into the driver's seat. Chris was still enamored enough with the West to despise such a foppish thing as a man riding in a buggy, so he went to his horse, mounted, and waved at Jim. "We'll meet you in town, Jim," he said and let out a shrill yelp as the horse tore out at full speed. Easy, upon seeing this, had said, "Come on. Let's don't let that dandy beat us, fellers." The crew all spurred their horses and took off, leaving a cloud of dust.

Reno chuckled softly. "Chris has become a good hand, Lillian. I never thought anybody would learn so quick to take to this life. It's hard on someone who didn't grow up with it."

Lillian turned and examined Reno, and her eyes were soft. "It's your doing, Jim." He attempted to deny it, but she quickly added, "It's true. If you hadn't come after Martin died and taken us in hand, I don't know where we'd be. In the poorhouse, I suppose."

Reno spoke to the horses, who began to trot. "Well, if we don't stop some of this rustling, we may be in the poorhouse yet," he observed. His eyes were always active, looking from point to point, a habit he had formed during his days in the Confederate army.

"Is it really that bad, Jim?"

"Bad enough, and it's gonna get worse. I thought we ought to get together with the other ranchers and see what we could do to stop it. But I don't know—these rustlers are pretty slick. They don't ever take big herds, just a few at a time. And by the time we find out they're gone, there are no tracks to follow."

Lillian put her hand on his arm, and her smile was brilliant. "You'll find them, Jim," she said confidently. "Nothing you put your hand to ever failed."

He gave her a startled glance, then shook his head. "That's what you think?" he asked wryly. "I could give you a long list of stuff I've tried that went flat busted."

It was a pleasant trip to town, although by the time they arrived, the sun was growing hot. Finally they pulled up in front of the plain white frame building with the small cross on top.

"Looks like a good crowd," Jim observed, casting his eyes over the wagons and buggies that were tied outside the small church. He helped Lillian to the ground, and they turned to go toward the church.

"Good morning, Lillian, Jim." They turned to find Sheriff Lige Benoit approaching them from where he had been standing in the shade. He came to stand before them, pulled off his gray Stetson, and asked idly, "Going to church, are you?"

"Why, yes, Sheriff Benoit," Lillian said. She smiled, and two dimples appeared in her cheeks. "Why don't you go with us?"

Benoit had been watching the crowd as they gathered for church, and the sight of Lillian in her pale blue dress had drawn him. He had admired her ever since she had come to town, and he had learned to respect the woman. But now he looked somewhat embarrassed, and he glanced down at the ground and shook his head. "Reckon the roof would fall in if I ever went inside that church."

Lillian said firmly, "I doubt that, Lige. Come along. Maybe we can get a seat up front where everybody can see us."

Reno grinned at Lige's anguished expression. He shook his head, saying, "You're trapped, Sheriff."

As they went inside, a mutter went over the crowd. Lige Benoit had never darkened the door of a church, as someone remarked audibly in Jim's hearing. They found a seat halfway to the front, and when Reno looked around, he saw all the crew propped like buzzards on a roost along the back row. Easy grinned at him and nodded, and beside Easy, Lee and Chris waved.

Even as they seated themselves, the mayor of the town stepped up on the platform and said, "We're going to have singing that'll lift the roof." He introduced the song leader, Dale Devaney. Devaney, the banker, was a large man, heavy, with small hazel eyes that missed nothing. He was, Jim Reno had discovered, a fervent Christian. *Strange thing for a banker,* Reno thought. *He's almost as demanding as Easy.* He had a fine tenor voice, and as they sang song after song, Jim's mind went back to the days of his youth, when he had sat in churches like this one and sung the same songs. Once, as they were singing "Amazing Grace," he felt himself grow suddenly remorseful and thought, *I've sure gotten away from any grace I might have had. . . .* Glancing at Lillian, he admired the peaceful expression on her face. *Some people, like Lillian and Mona, have sure got a joy in the Lord. I wonder if I'll ever find it.* He began to sing again, and after the song service, he watched as the pastor rose and approached the pulpit. Reverend Allen Danforth was a new pastor. He was twenty-eight years old, and as Jim studied him, he saw a man of average height with light brown hair rebelliously curly and a pair of piercing brown eyes. He was not handsome but had strong, masculine features. He had seen to the conversion of many in and around Banning—Easy included—in his few months in town. Danforth was an idealistic young man, the church had found, and this had created some difficulty. To Allen Danforth being a Christian was a seven-day-a-week job, and those who had attempted to relegate it to the Sabbath found themselves up against some direct and scathing denunciations as the young pastor faced them.

But Danforth was smiling this morning as he said, "We're glad to have all of you here. I invite all of you now to turn to your Bibles, and we will begin with Romans 3:23, which says

plainly, 'All have sinned and come short of the glory of God.'"
He looked out over the congregation and let the silence run
on, then repeated the verse, accentuating the first word "'*All*
have sinned'—that doesn't leave much doubt, does it, friends?
That includes everybody in this house."

A sudden "Hallelujah! Tell 'em, Preacher!" startled Reno,
and he grinned slightly. He was accustomed, for the most part,
to Easy's habit of helping the preacher with continual shouts
of "Amen," "Hallelujah," and "Go to it." But he was aware that
others were not yet so comfortable with his spirit of enthusi-
asm. Nevertheless, the sermon went on, and Reno listened
carefully. He glanced from time to time over across the room
to where Lew Meade and his bride, Mona, sat, and he wondered about Jason. The earth seemed to have swallowed him
up since he had come to live at the Slash A. Reno had seen the
tension mount on the faces of Lew and Mona, and although he
had not seen Simon, Mona had said last week, "It's not working, Jim. Jason—Lone Wolf—takes no part in the ranch. He's
gone most of the time, and when he does see Simon, he
doesn't have anything to say." Reno had tried to encourage her
that night, but there had seemed to be little he could say.

Jim Reno had heard many sermons—and he'd heard better. But as he sat on the hard seat he began to experience a
strange sensation. As Danforth read the Scripture and commented on it, Reno began to feel . . . weak. There was no other
word for it, and when he tried to tell himself he was acting
poorly, he realized that his hands were trembling.

Didn't think anything in the world could do that to me! he
thought. He became disoriented, and he was filled with a name-
less dread, a fear that caught in his stomach. Reno had been
afraid many times, but those were times when he was in physi-

cal danger. Now he was sitting in a church, safe from bullets, arrows, and stampedes—yet he was *afraid.*

I must be getting sick. Maybe I've got the flu. I've got to get out of here!

But then he began to understand. The fear was not something that he could run from, for it had to do with God. He had heard about *conviction* often enough to understand that this was what was filling him with a weakness. And he was acutely aware that it was when Danforth was speaking of the Lord Jesus Christ that the feeling was worse.

"Jesus died for all people," Danforth proclaimed. "But he would have died for you if you were the only lost person in the world. His love for you is that powerful! . . ."

The sermon went on for what seemed to be a long time, but the preacher's words faded away, and Jim was startled when a question came to him so clearly that he could not mistake it: *Will you have Jesus Christ as your Lord and Savior?*

Reno's face grew clammy, and his hands trembled so violently that he gripped them to hide the tremors. Again and again the question came, and an agony pressed down on his spirit.

I—I think this is my last chance, he thought numbly. *I've run from God for years, but he's caught up with me!*

And then he heard singing and looked up to see with shock that the sermon was over and the congregation was standing. He rose slowly, and he knew that he must give an answer to the question that continued to echo in his mind: *Will you have Jesus Christ as your Lord and Savior?*

As the congregation filed out, Jim walked over to the pastor and asked unsteadily, "Reckon I could talk to you in private, Reverend Danforth?"

Danforth gave Reno a searching look. When he looked in Reno's eyes, he felt deep joy. "Of course, Jim. Go into the back room. I'll finish greeting the folks and then be right with you."

Lillian stopped to shake hands with the preacher, and Lige Benoit hung back in embarrassment. But Allen Danforth would not permit that. "It's good to see you here, Sheriff," he said. When Benoit took the preacher's hand, he found out that the preacher had a grip such as he had rarely felt. He met the pressure with his own and grinned sheepishly. "That was a good sermon, Preacher. No doubt in my mind about who you meant."

Danforth had been stern part of the time during the message, but now there was a genuine gentleness in his eyes. "I meant all of us. We all need God."

"I reckon that's right," Lige said, and he moved away, Lillian going with him.

Danforth wanted to go to Reno at once, but he covered his impatience well. Danforth had learned to appreciate Reno and had talked with him about his own soul. He had found Reno to be open and yet somehow reluctant. There was a wall built around Jim Reno that had never been broken down, and Danforth had thought, *He'll have to be broken by something big before Jim will ever get saved.*

Mona and Lew came up, and Mona, after greeting the preacher, said, "I hear the new schoolmaster has been hired. When's he coming?"

Danforth shook his head. "It's not a he, Mrs. Meade. It's a lady—Miss Sharon Templeton. She'll be here next week."

"She better bring a big stick," Lew said. "Some of those young fellows in that schoolroom are nearly as big as I am. They'll give her a hard time."

"You'll have to go over and give 'em a lesson in manners," Danforth said with a grin. Then he asked seriously, "What about Jason?"

A cloud immediately touched the eyes of Lew Meade. He shook his head and bit his lip. "No good, Reverend. I've tried everything I know—but it is impossible to get next to that man."

Mona took her husband's arm. "You'd think he might at least try to become a part of the family, but he doesn't, not ever. He doesn't eat with the family half the time. He's always out hunting or fishing."

Danforth felt constrained to say, "You've got to remember, Mona—and you too, Lew—that's been his life. Indians don't carry watches. They do what they want to do. When they get hungry, they eat; when they get sleepy, they sleep. Their whole life is like a stream that meanders here and there. They're just not much for planning."

Lew stared at him then nodded. "I guess that's right." He shook his head almost angrily. "One thing he got from being an Indian is that stone face of his. It's impossible to know what he's thinking!"

The Meades left, and finally Danforth was able to go to the back room. He saw that Jim was standing straight as an arrow but that his eyes were filled with doubt. "Sit down," the minister said quietly. "Let's talk about how you're going to let God have your life. . . ."

They talked in that room for over two hours, for Reno was fearful that he'd sinned too greatly to receive God's forgiveness. Slowly, line upon line and precept upon precept, Danforth used the Scriptures to bring Reno into an understanding of God's grace.

Finally Reno looked up—and there were tears glistening in his eyes. "All right, Preacher. How do I do it?"

"If you believe that Jesus died for your sins, then all you need to do is ask God to forgive you and to take control of your life. That's your part, Jim. It's God's part to do the saving. Now shall we pray?"

The two knelt, and they were not long on their knees. Danforth was skilled at leading this sort of prayer, and soon Reno stood up and smiled. "I've done it, Preacher! Something—something has happened to me!"

Standing up, Danforth asked Reno a few questions and then said, "Jim, Jesus Christ has come into your life. Thank God for his grace!"

Reno left the small room in the church and for the rest of the day rode the countryside. He paused to read the Bible that Danforth had given him, and he was shocked at how *different* the Scripture seemed. Finally he turned and headed for the ranch, thinking, *Nothing's ever going to be the same again!*

And it was not the same. Reno told of his conversion and his determination to serve God, and everyone at the ranch rejoiced over his new resolve. He began studying the Bible under the pastor and kept to himself a great deal, but those who knew him best saw that he had a calm joy and satisfaction that had been lacking in his life. *Wish I'd done it years ago,* Reno thought more than once. *But I thank God he didn't give up on me.*

Later the next week, on Tuesday, Reno took time off from Sun Ranch and rode over to Slash A. He found that Jason had gone hunting over somewhere in the foothills and took off at once to find him. He rode through the uprising hills filled with scrub brush and sharp points of rocks until he came to a creek. *Pretty good chance he'll be somewhere along this creek,* he thought, *waitin' for the animals to come to water.* He meandered along slowly, thinking about many things. About Jack Bronte up in the hills, stripping the ranchers of their cattle and laughing at them. About Lillian, who for all her brightness was lonely and unhappy. About Lee, who was growing up and had no roots except what had been provided here at Sun Ranch for the past year. He was deep in thought when a voice called out, and he looked up to see Lone Wolf step out from behind a tree.

Reno shoved his hat back as he pulled Duke up. "Good thing you're friendly," he said. "A fellow could loose his scalp hoofing along like this if he wasn't in friendly country."

Lone Wolf had learned to accept the gentle jibes that Jim had given him about Indian things on their trip back to Slash A. He was not wearing a hat, and his dark auburn hair gleamed in the sunlight, the braid proudly hanging down his back. He wore only a vest over a pair of fawn-colored trousers, and a pair of finely beaded moccasins completed his costume. In his hands he had a bow and over his back a quiver full of arrows. Coming forward, he said, "Are you lost, Reno?"

"Nope. I took a day off." He slipped off Duke's back, stretched, then said, "Some time ago Lincoln emancipated all the slaves. Lately I've been working like a slave, so I decided to do what old Abe did and emancipated myself for the day." He looked down at the bow and said, "Get anything yet?"

"Not yet."

"Mind if I join you?"

"Sure."

Reno did not mount his horse but led him along until they

got to a meadow formed inside the trees. Pulling out a pair of hobbles, he put them on Duke's feet and pulled the saddle off. "Now there's water and some grass. You have yourself a feast while I go have some fun."

He turned and followed Jason out of the glade, and the tall young man led him, with a smooth stride, deeper into the woods. "Should have worn my low heel boots," Jim complained. "These high heels were not made for stalking game." For the next two hours the two moved through the woods, finally taking up a stand next to a large pool that had been formed. They talked little, and Jim knew that Lone Wolf was wondering why he had come. They were still-hunting now and had sat absolutely motionless for the better part of an hour when a big buck stepped out from a group of small poplar trees. Jim had brought his rifle, but he nudged Jason, flickering his eyes at the bow. Jason, in one smooth motion, raised the bow, pulled it to full tension, and loosed the arrow that hissed through the air. The buck responded too late, and the arrow caught him right behind the left foreleg. He snorted, coughed, and ran off through the brush, but Lone Wolf said, "He won't get far."

"That was a good shot," Jim said. He looked at the bow and shook his head. "I couldn't hit a barn with one of those things."

"I learned when I was very small," he said. They rose and followed the blood track of the deer and less than a hundred yards away found him dead on the ground. "If you want to wait, I'll go get Duke and we can pack him out."

"Might as well carry him." Lone Wolf removed the arrow, cleaned it, stuck it into the quiver, and then stripped the quiver from his shoulders. Handing the quiver and the bow to Jim,

Lone Wolf reached down and with no effort at all picked up the buck and slung him over his shoulders. Reno lifted his eyebrows, impressed, for it was a heavy animal and yet seemed to have no weight at all for the young warrior.

He did not comment, however, and the two got back to Duke and tied the buck on behind the horse. Lone Wolf then went to get his own horse and soon came back. The two men rode along, heading back toward the ranch, and Reno still said nothing. He had decided that there was no point in urging the young man to act like a white man. *I'll just be as friendly as I can. Maybe he'll see that all white folks aren't varmints,* he thought.

They had circled around through the hills until, as they went back, they had to pass close to town. "Might as well go in and get some shells while I'm here," Reno said. "You mind, Lone Wolf?"

"No." Lone Wolf, nevertheless, looked somewhat apprehensive.

Jim understood. *He's still not sure about this white man's world.* "Won't take long," he said.

They pulled into Banning and went directly to the general store, which was owned by Kyle Poindexter. Before they went in, Jim said, "There's Sheriff Benoit. I've got to see him for a minute. Tie your horse up, and I'll be in in a minute."

Jason nodded, tied his horse alongside Duke, and looked at the store. He mounted the steps, his moccasined feet making no sound, passed through the door, and looked around at the interior. It was much larger than the trading post he had been to near the Sioux territory, and the shelves lined with groceries of all kinds, hardware, and cloth caught his eye. He moved over to where a glass case contained a row of revolvers and several rifles. They looked beautifully done to him, and he stood there silently, admiring the workmanship. He had forgotten about the man who had watched him come in, and then a voice came right behind his ear. "Injun, you can go outside. I don't want you in here."

Jason whirled, his light blue eyes startling against his coppery face. He looked entirely dangerous, and although he made no move toward the revolver on his thigh or the knife at his side, Kyle Poindexter took a step back and then went behind the counter, where he kept a gun. "I told you," he said, reaching down, "Get out of my store."

At that moment, Jim entered with Lew Meade, whom he had met while talking to Benoit. The two men stopped, each of them taking in the situation. Anger ran through Reno like a white iron tingling his nerves. Deliberately he quieted himself, and then moved over to stand beside Jason. "A little trouble, Poindexter?"

Poindexter was a large, heavy man. He was outspoken in his criticism of Indians, often quoting the well-known dictum *The only good Indian is a dead Indian.* He lifted his head and said sourly, "Some of my folks were killed by Indians."

At that moment Lew stepped forward, and one look at him told Poindexter he had more on his hands than he could handle. Lew was only a little shorter than Jason. He had been considered by many as far from serious, but he looked serious—and frightening—enough to suit the storekeeper.

Lew bit back an angry retort then said conversationally, "Well, I've always thought your prices were high, Poindexter. I guess we can take our business over to Seven Pines to Jimmy Malvern's store. It's a little farther, but it'll be worth the trouble."

Reno said, "I guess we can go together, Lew. I'm sure Lillian wouldn't want to do business with a man who would insult a neighbor's son."

"Son?" Poindexter looked around warily, and then he remembered. "Oh." He grew tense as he realized his mistake. "You're Simon Meade's boy." A forced smile came to his lips, and he said, "Well, now, I'll have to apologize. I didn't know you—"

"You didn't know I was white?" Jason asked quietly. "If I cut my braid off, will you let me in this store?" He turned and walked out of the store.

Lew stared at Poindexter. "You're a fine specimen, Poindexter." He, too, turned and walked away.

As Jim followed, Poindexter began to yell, "Wait a minute now. Can't a man make a mistake? I didn't know he wasn't an Indian! . . ." But his words fell on empty air, and he walked over and angrily slammed his fist against the wall.

EIGHT
New Schoolmarm

A gauzy spiral of dust marked the approach of the stagecoach. Allen Danforth had left the church and walked down to the general store, which served as a stagecoach station. He watched eagerly as the stagecoach crested a hill and headed for town. The young minister had worked hard to replace the schoolteacher who had left, a drunken Irishman who had few qualifications to begin with and who had to be forcibly removed at the behest of Danforth.

The search for a teacher for the school had been arduous. Danforth had served as unofficial chairman of a committee of one to bring names to the members of the community and had been successful, finally, in getting an applicant with what he considered the proper credentials. He would have preferred a man, but none appeared, and at the urging of an old college and school friend of his, he had written to Sharon Templeton, who had served successfully in Chicago as a teacher in a small school. He had been impressed with her letter, which was sensible and brief and which had presented her considerable qualifications without boasting. She had achieved high grades at her college and had good recommendations from the community where she had taught school for two years; all of them were glowing with praise of her ability as a teacher.

The small funnel of dust grew larger, and Danforth moved over on the boardwalk in front of the store, waiting for it to pull in. The team finally rounded the corner, the driver sawing on the reins and calling out, "Whoa, there, blast you!" He slammed on the brakes, bringing the stagecoach to a shuddering halt, and then spat an amber stream into the dust.

Allen Danforth stepped forward at once, opened the door, and saw that there was only one woman along with three men. She got up and stepped to the door, and he held his hand up to assist her. He was surprised to see that she wore a veil over half of her face. Her hand was firm and warm, and he could tell that she was an attractive young lady. "Miss Templeton," he said as she stepped to the ground. He took off his hat and smiled, adding, "I'm glad to see you. My name is Allen Danforth."

"Reverend Danforth, is it?" The voice was quiet and assured and rather deep for a woman. Behind the veil was a pair of steady eyes.

"Yes. I'm the pastor of the church." He glanced at the stagecoach and said, "If you'll show me your luggage, I'll see that it gets taken to your room."

"That trunk and the three valises." She indicated the luggage, and he lifted them, putting them on the boardwalk.

"My buggy is just down the street. Let me go get it, and I'll take you to your room."

He turned, walked quickly down the street, stepped into the buggy, and drove it down to where she stood waiting. She was wearing a pale green dress, which Danforth considered rather flamboyant for a schoolteacher, and a small, dark green hat that was perched up on top of her black hair, as black as hair could possibly be. Stepping out, he loaded her trunk and valises, then moved forward handing her up into the buggy. Moving quickly, he circled the wagon, climbed into the seat, and taking up the reins, spoke to the horse. As they made their way down the street, he saw her looking carefully at the town and said apologetically, "Not much like Chicago, is it, Miss Templeton?"

"No, it isn't."

He could make nothing of her voice. It was not critical, and certainly there was nothing to fault in it. He was a little surprised at her brevity but considered that perhaps in a strange place, so far removed from her ordinary settings and locale, she was a little overwhelmed.

He chatted easily, taking up the conversation and pointing out various businesses, discussing the school and the students, and telling her, of course, of his interest in the school. They drove to the end of town, and when they left she said, glancing back, "We're leaving town?"

"Yes. The school is right down the road, and you'll be staying, if you approve, with a family that lives just across the road. It'll be convenient for you." He paused to give her time to comment, but she did not. Finally he lifted his hand and said, "There's the school. The old one burned down, so we built a new one two years ago."

The school was a square building, freshly coated with white paint, which Danforth had seen to. It sat in an opening surrounded by some tall trees.

"It looks very nice," Miss Templeton said. She turned toward him, adding, "As a matter of fact, it looks almost exactly as I had pictured it."

"Have you ever been west, Miss Templeton?"

"No farther west than the Mississippi River." There was a slight hesitation there, then she added, "I hope I'll be able to find my way here. It's sometimes difficult for strangers to move into a different territory."

"Oh, I'm sure you will," Danforth said quickly. "We are nowhere near the size of a city like Chicago. Would you like to see the school before I take you to your room to meet the Middletons?"

"That would be nice."

He pulled the buggy up, got out and tied the horse, walked around, and handed her down. She was, he saw, slightly below middle height and very well formed and shapely. He wondered about the veil, for it was somewhat unusual. *Probably Eastern fashion, I guess,* he thought. They walked to the school, and he opened the door and stepped back to let her enter. When they were inside, he waved at the benches and said, "Everything is in fairly good shape. We had a good carpenter make the desks, and your desk up there was donated by a prominent family here. It's solid walnut and has plenty of drawer space."

The woman walked forward and ran her hand across the surface of the desk, on which rested a ruler, a small jar full of pencils, several writing tablets, and a vase of flowers. She smiled then, saying, "It's very nice. Much better than I expected."

The two of them walked around, and he showed her the well and the outdoor privies, expecting her to blush somewhat at that, but she showed no more than ordinary interest. Finally he said, "I know you must be tired. Let's go meet the Middletons and you can rest."

They went back to the buggy and got in, then drove three hundred yards down the road, where Danforth pulled up in front of a two-story frame house. "You'll like the Middletons," he said, helping her out. "Mrs. Middleton is a widow with two children. Her husband died last year, and she's been having a hard time, so I thought your board might help her."

Once again she did not speak but nodded slightly. When they went up on the porch, Mrs. Middleton came outside to meet them. "Good evening, Reverend Danforth. And this must be Miss Templeton." Mrs. Middleton was an attractive woman of thirty years of age, and she had a smile for her new boarder. "I've got your room all ready, Miss Templeton," she said. "Let me show it to you."

"I'll get your luggage," Allen Danforth said quickly. He went back to the buggy, moved the trunk and the valises to the porch, then waited until Mrs. Middleton came outside. "Would you carry her things up, Reverend?"

"Where are the children?" Danforth asked. Bobby Middleton, age ten, and his eight-year-old sister, Lorena, were favorites of Danforth, who loved all children. Usually they were underfoot, but he had not seen them today.

"Fishing down at the pond. Let me hold the door for you."

Danforth carried the heavy trunk up on one shoulder to the top of the stairs and moved down the hall to where he saw an open door. Glancing in, he saw the woman standing by the window. She turned and said, "Come in, please." He stepped inside, put the trunk down beside the dresser, then said, "I'll go get the rest of the valises."

"Please don't bother," she said. But he insisted, and soon he was back up and put the valises down.

"I expect you're tired," he said. "But as soon as you're

rested, I would like to talk with you about some plans I have for improving the school."

She appeared not to have heard his words. She stood still, and she was observing him carefully. Turning her head so the right side of her face was to Danforth, she slowly reached up, removed the hat and the veil, which seemed to be attached to the hat, and put them down on the dresser. She was, he noticed, a very beautiful young woman. Her black hair was set off by a pair of light green eyes, a most striking combination, and her lips were wide and well shaped. Her face was an oval, and her complexion was flawless. He said, "Of course, I don't want to—"

At that moment she turned her face the other way. Danforth hesitated only slightly, and then said, "—bother you with details, but I know you'll be interested."

He had been taken off guard by the left side of the woman's face. The right side, which was so flawless, gave no hint of a scar that traced its way down through her black hair, where the hair had grown white up over her left ear. It ran jaggedly down her face, just in front of her ear, and ended just above her jawbone. It had been such a savage wound that it pulled her left eye slightly shut.

Danforth, desperately aware that she had noticed his hesitation, began to make a hasty withdrawal. "Well, I'll leave you now, Miss Templeton."

"I see you noticed my scar."

Danforth blinked in shock and stood there speechless, not knowing how to answer that.

"It doesn't affect my teaching in any way, Reverend."

She was watching him carefully, and when her face was turned toward him, all he could see was the single, small line of white that scored her black hair. Her eyes held a peculiar expression, and there was something close to bitterness in the set of her well-shaped mouth as she added, "It comes as a shock to most people, and sooner or later some of the children will think up names to call me when I'm strict with them."

Danforth licked his lips and said, "I'm sorry if—"

"Oh no. You mustn't be sorry. It's natural. Everyone does exactly what you did. I usually wear a veil when I'm traveling. It makes things a little easier. But now that I'm here, there's no point in it. People will just have to get used to my deformity."

"Oh, not a deformity!" Danforth exclaimed vehemently.

"You think not?"

"Why, of course not. How did it—?" he stammered and then said quickly, "Of course it's none of my business. I hope that you won't be subjected to any embarrassment."

"I will be," she said calmly. And then she did smile, and when she smiled, she made an attractive picture. Her green eyes glinted with a perverse humor as she said, "One thing about being scarred like this, no one ever forgets you. You may forget a hundred people, but you'll never forget me, will you, Reverend Danforth?"

"I should not have done that in any case," he said stoutly. Danforth was shaken and said, "I trust you'll be comfortable. Services are held every Sunday morning, and I'd like to invite you to come."

Sharon Templeton looked at the minister and let the silence run on. Then she said rather curtly, "I don't attend services." Then she said, "Thank you for your help. I'll be glad to talk with you about the school at your convenience."

Danforth nodded, mumbled a farewell, and left. As he left the house he said, "I've never felt so foolish in all my life. What difference can a scar make? She's still a beautiful woman." But he knew that it did make a difference, at least to her.

★ ★ ★

"Doggone it! I don't see how you do that."

Lee was glaring at the fish that lay flopping on the grass. He turned his eyes on Lone Wolf. He had tried time and again to do what Lone Wolf seemed to do so easily. He lay on his stomach, extended his arm and immersed it down to the shoulder, and was able to grab fish and throw them clear.

Jason sat up, grinned at the boy, and said, "You have to be smarter than the fish, Lee."

Reno was sitting with his back against the tree. He laughed softly, saying, "That's what they say about training mules. You gotta be smarter than the mule." He got to his feet then, saying, "You got enough fish there to feed half the town. I've got to get back before the bank closes."

"Oh, just let me try one more time," Lee pleaded. But Reno was adamant, and the three gathered up the sack full of fish that they had caught, Lee's with a hook and line, and much larger ones that Jason had tickled—at least so he said.

All the way into town Lee shot question after question at Jason about the life he had led, and Reno rode quietly, enjoying the scene. It was the loosest, most relaxed mood that he had seen Lone Wolf in, and he knew that it was good for Lee as well.

They were half a mile from town when Reno broke into Lee's steady fusillade of questions, saying, "Look, there's the school. I wouldn't be surprised if that's the new teacher out by the well."

"Oh, there ain't no school yet, not for another three days," Lee said apprehensively.

"That might be," Reno said. A grin shaped his broad lips, and he shoved his hat back. "But I think we better stop and give her a warning about what a terrible fellow you are."

"Oh, Jim!"

But, though Lee protested, Reno led the pair into the schoolyard, where they all dismounted.

Lee and Jason stayed by the hitching rail while Jim strolled around the edge of the building to where a young woman was struggling to bring a bucket of water up out of the well. "Let me help you with that, Miss."

The woman turned around to face him. Reno saw the scar on her face, but he let nothing show in his expression. Reaching over, he pulled the full, heavy, wooden bucket to the top, unhooked it, and said, "Are you going inside with this?"

"Yes, if you don't mind."

"I'm Jim Reno."

"My name is Sharon Templeton."

"Glad to know you, Miss Templeton. I've got a boy—not my own, but one I'm lookin' out for. He's fifteen, and I wanted you to meet him before school started." He hesitated, then said, "He's had a pretty rough time, and I'm all he's got in the way of a family. If he gives you problems, I'm the one you should come to."

"I'll certainly do that, Mr. Reno. Where is he?"

"Around front. Oh, by the way," Reno said, "there's another friend of mine that could use a little help. He's a grown man, but he hasn't had any chance at learning. He can read, and his mother taught him to write a little bit, but—"

"I'll be glad to help if I can."

"That'll be fine," he said with a grin. "I'll come and chop wood to pay their tuition."

"You don't have to do that." She smiled, and there was a sprightly attractiveness about the young woman. They walked around the corner of the school, and Jim called, "Come here and meet the teacher."

Lee came first, with Lone Wolf loitering behind. Jim said, "I told Miss Templeton what an excellent scholar you are, Lee. Don't let me down, now."

Lee ducked his head and flushed. "Well, I'm not all that much, I guess."

Sharon Templeton smiled at him and drew his eyes upward. "I'm sure we'll have a good time, Lee."

And then Reno said, "And this is Lone Wolf."

He was watching the woman's face and did not miss what happened. She lifted her eyes with a smile and then saw Lone Wolf. He never looked more like an Indian than he did at that moment. He was wearing a black hat without a crease, a simple vest that exposed his chest and arms, tanned copper, a pair of doeskin britches, and moccasins. Jim saw the light go out of the woman's face, and she said shortly, "How do you do?"

Lone Wolf read the dislike in her eyes. He nodded without speaking, and even Lee sensed the tension. Reno said at once, "Well, we'll be moving along. I'll appreciate what you can do, and we're glad to welcome you to town."

Sharon Templeton turned to him, but the light was gone out of her eyes, and her lips were tight. "Good to meet you," she replied in a spare tone, then turned and walked into the building.

As the three went back to their horses, Lee said, "What in the world's wrong with her?"

Lone Wolf looked at him and said simply, "She hates Indians."

"Oh, Lone Wolf, that ain't so." But when he looked at Jim, he saw no assurance in Reno's eyes.

"Well, I don't like her, then, and I ain't going to her old school!"

"Yes you are, Lee," Reno said, and the tone of his voice was firm. The three rode silently out of town.

NINE
Lee Brings a Visitor

Simon Meade picked at the food that his daughter-in-law had set before him, studying the face of his youngest son. He had done little else for weeks. Lone Wolf spoke almost not at all, except in answer to questions. In an attempt to draw the young man out, Simon said, "Lew tells me you can ride any rough bronc on the place, Jason. That'll come in helpful."

Lone Wolf lifted his light blue eyes toward his father, shrugged, and said almost inaudibly, "Not too hard." Then he said with some emotion, "Would you please honor my wishes and call me by my Sioux name."

Simon grew even more uncomfortable. "I'm sorry, Son. You've always been Jason to me. I just can't get used to calling you by another name." He noticed a look of anger beginning to form on his son's face, so he added, "But I'll try . . . , Lone Wolf."

Lone Wolf only nodded.

Lew Meade, seated at the other end of the long table, said nothing. He glanced at Mona and gave a slight shake of his head. He thought, *He hasn't done anything but ride a few horses since he's been here—not a bit of work. And we can use every bit of help we can get.* However, Lew had purposed not to say one critical word to his brother, and now he said cheerfully, "Well, I've got to go down to the east pasture. We've got some stock down there we need to move to lower ground." He got up, walked over to the window, and looked out. "Still looks nice enough, but I can tell the days are starting to get cooler. All the signs point to a bad winter this year." A frown worked its way onto his face. "I hope the woolly bears and squirrels are wrong."

Mona moved to fill Lone Wolf's coffee cup, and he looked up quickly and gave her a careful examination. *He still feels so out of place,* she thought as he nodded briefly, saying nothing. She wasn't comfortable either, as his long silences and extremely brief remarks proved to be very distracting.

Lew moved toward the door, followed by Lone Wolf, who drank his coffee quickly and set the cup on the table on his way out. Lew noted that Jason said nothing and merely nodded toward his father and Mona. Jason knew that when he stepped outside they would be speaking of him, but he could not bring himself to open up. He waited until Lew and the crew had mounted up and ridden out, and then he slipped a hackamore on his own horse and leaped on its back. His habit of riding bareback was another thing that set him apart from the rest of the punchers. Baldy Sims, the oldest puncher on the place, had remarked to Zeno Pounders, "It ain't *natural,* Zeno! It's his heathen training—that's what it is!"

"I reckon you're right. It looks like a man could change when he comes to live with white folks."

The two men had summed up the sentiment of the entire valley. Most people had at least made an attempt to welcome

Simon Meade's younger son into their fellowship, but when he had ignored them and gone his own way, retaining much of his Indian appearance, they had shrugged and turned a cold shoulder to him.

Lone Wolf enjoyed the horse that his father had given him, a sleek bay stallion with plenty of bottom and capable of a burst of speed such as he had never enjoyed in a horse. For two hours he rode to the hills, carrying only a bow and arrow and the knife in his belt. He was fairly proficient with a rifle but chose not to use the six-shooter on his hip.

Later, when it was almost noon, he pulled into the dooryard of the Sun Ranch and at once was greeted by Lee Morgan. "Hey, Lone Wolf," the young man called, and he ran across the yard to meet him. "Guess what? Rustlers hit our herd last night."

Slipping off the horse, Lone Wolf studied the young man and then asked, "Did the crew go after them?"

"Yeah. Jim took all the men we had, but he said it wouldn't do much good. After that rain we had yesterday, all the tracks would be washed out. Too bad you wasn't here. I bet you coulda tracked 'em, couldn't you've, Lone Wolf?"

The obvious admiration in Lee Morgan was the one bright spot in Lone Wolf's return to the white world. With this young man, at least, he could unbend, for there was no craft, guile, or subtlety in Lee Morgan. Jason smiled at the implication that he could track anything and shook his head. "Not sure," he said. "My father could." He meant his father in the tribe and caught himself. "Running Bear, I mean, could track an eagle over bare rocks, I think."

Lee said, "Come on! You're gonna give me a lesson with the bow and arrow. You promised."

A smile creased the lips of Lone Wolf such as had not been seen by any of the adults in this world, and at once he went with the boy to the edge of the woods. There they set up a target, and for the next hour Lone Wolf enjoyed himself immensely. Finally Lee said in disgust, "I can't hit nothin' with this."

"It takes practice," Lone Wolf encouraged. "You're very strong and you have steady hands." It was a good time for Lee despite his lack of success, and finally he said haltingly, "I've got a favor to ask of you, Lone Wolf."

"What is it?"

Lee ducked his head and drew a figure in the dust with his toe. He bit his lip as if reluctant to speak and finally shrugged. "Well, you won't do it, I know. But tomorrow is my day at school to bring something."

"Bring something?"

"Yeah. Every day the teacher, Miss Templeton, lets one student bring something and show it to the class and tell about it. Like yesterday, Frankie Tompson, he brought this musket— his grandpa's musket—that was used in the Revolutionary War, and he showed us all how it worked. He didn't shoot it, but it was interesting." He scowled and said, "Everybody brought something interesting, but I ain't got nothin' to take. Unless . . ."

Lone Wolf looked down at the boy and felt a warmth, for he longed to do something to help the young man. "You and I are brothers," he said and watched the warm flush that suf- fused Lee's cheeks. "Brothers help one another. What do you want to take? My bow?"

"Well, more than that," Lee said reluctantly. Then he began to talk rapidly. "Gee, Lone Wolf, if you'd just go with me and show everybody how to shoot, they ain't never seen nothin' like that. Why, you can hit *anything!* And it would be like nobody else has brought. . . ."

Jason stiffened when he heard the boy's request, but as he watched the pleading expression in the young man's eyes, he thought, *What do I have to lose? No one can say anything about me they haven't already said.* He waited till Lee ran out of steam, then put his hand on his shoulder. "I will go with you," he said.

Lee's joy knew no bounds, and he grabbed Jason's arm and dragged him toward the house. Lillian had been watching the two as they approached, and when she came out, she was subjected to Lee's excitement. He burst forth, "Mrs. Reynolds, Lone Wolf—he's gonna go to school with me and give a demonstration of bow shootin'. Ain't that somethin'?"

Lillian smiled at the boy, and when she looked up at Lone Wolf, he saw that the smile did not change as it did with some. "How nice of you, Lone Wolf," she said warmly. "I'll have to give you a reward for that. The men are gone, and I've got enough food cooked for half a dozen. You have supper and then spend the night."

It was a pleasant night for Lone Wolf, perhaps the best he had had since he had come to live with his father. Lee made no real demands on him, except to tell stories and to teach him things, which the young man received great pleasure in doing. The two sat there after supper, Jason telling stories of his boyhood, of hunts, of raids, and not noticing that Lillian was listening just as avidly as the boy.

Finally she broke into Lee's conversation, saying, "Lee, it's getting late. You'd better go to bed. Come early for breakfast, and you can eat with Lone Wolf and me."

"Come on," Lee said to his friend. "You can sleep in the bunkhouse with me."

Jason rose and paused when Lillian said, "I was fascinated by your stories, Lone Wolf." She ceased to smile, then said, "I haven't ever told you, but I grieve over the loss of your family and your people. I hope you will find a place here with all of us. Think of this as your home, if you will."

Jason blinked in surprise, then said in a muted tone, "Thank you, Mrs. Reynolds," and turned and went out to the bunkhouse with Lee.

The yellow bar of the late-September sunlight came through Sharon's window and fell across her face. She slowly came out of sleep, stirred softly, but did not open her eyes. It had gotten to be a habit with her that she did not get up at once but lay in bed pulling her thoughts together. She lay there quietly, thinking mostly of the school and of the students. Finally she arose and went to wash her face and fix her hair. Pouring fresh water out of the pitcher into a basin, she lathered a cloth with a bar of soap. Briefly she looked up into the mirror, her hand half-raised to her right cheek. The morning light caught her full across the left side of her face, and she froze in the position, staring at the white streak in her black hair and the jagged scar that ran down her face. Motionless, she stood there, her eyes fixed on her features, and then slowly she began to wash her face. *You'd think after all this time, I'd be accustomed to seeing what I look like. . . .*

Although the wound had been inflicted years before, there were still times, especially when she rose and was sleepy, when she forgot and was shocked when she saw the damage. As she continued to wash her face and then began to dress her hair, her lips drew into a tight line, and she avoided looking at the mirror any more than necessary. Finally, she dressed and went downstairs to breakfast with the Middleton family.

"Hello, Miss Sharon," Bobby said. At the age of ten, he was a fine-looking boy with red hair and bright blue eyes. He was very fond of Sharon, as was his sister, Lorena.

"Good morning, Bobby. Good morning, Lorena." Sharon smiled at them. As she sat down, she automatically turned her face away from them, slightly to the left. It was a habitual gesture that she was not aware of. Mrs. Middleton put the breakfast before her and chatted amiably. When they were finished and Sharon rose to go, she went over and put her hand on Sharon's arm. "I'm so glad you've come to teach the school," she said with a wide smile. "Bobby and Lorena just love you; they work their hearts out for you."

"They're good students," Sharon said. "And I'm grateful to you for furnishing a home, Ann. It's been good for me."

Ann Middleton hesitated then said, "You'd have more friends if you'd open up a little bit, Sharon." She hesitated then said, "Why don't you come to the church social with me?"

"Thank you. I'll think about it."

Ann knew she had stepped over some invisible line. She saw the slight hardening of the young woman's features and said quickly, "When you come back after school, I'll teach you how to bake a special kind of pie, as my mother taught me."

"That would be nice." She turned and walked out of the door and was joined by Bobby and Lorena. The three of them walked to school, where she could see the students already gathered and playing in the yard. When she got there, they came to swarm around her, and for that moment she was happy. She thought, *If I could just keep children around me and never see adults—how happy I'd be! Children accept just about anybody.* And then she said, "All right, Bobby, go ring the bell. Time for school."

She went inside and heard Bobby clanging the bell with gusto, and then the children filed in. Most of them were young children, although several were in their middle teens. Bobby Epps, at sixteen, was the oldest student, and at six feet four inches, he towered over Sharon as well as everyone else. He was, however, a mild-mannered young man and had given no problems.

Sharon began with the usual preliminaries and then suddenly looked over the room. "Lee's not here," she remarked.

Mary Sims said, "I bet he's staying away because he didn't have anything to bring and show us."

"I'm sure that's not so," Sharon said quickly. As she spoke she glanced up, for the sound of a horse approaching had caught her ears. Lee was one of those who always rode to school, and she smiled, saying, "This is probably Lee here."

She looked down at the desk, going over the grade book, heard steps as someone entered, and glanced up, a smile on her lips—which immediately faded.

Lee burst out in excitement, "Look, Miss Templeton. You said to bring something interesting. Well, I brought my friend, Lone Wolf. He's lived with the Indians, and he can hit anything with an arrow. Can we go outside so he can show us?"

Jason had entered behind Lee. He had put on a pair of blue denim pants made by Levi Strauss and a white shirt, but he still wore the moccasins, and the dark auburn braid still trailed down his back. He ignored the buzz that went around the young people and kept his bright blue eyes fixed on the woman seated at the desk. The moment she looked at him, he saw her face pale, and she moved her head slightly. He was astute enough to realize that she turned her head in a pitiful attempt to hide the scar, and he wondered why.

"Can we, can we, Miss Templeton?" the students began to cry out, and Sharon knew that there was no way out.

"Quiet, class!" She waited for silence and then said evenly, "I think that would be very nice, Lee. Are you ready now, Lone Wolf?"

"Yes." Lone Wolf was surprised, for he had expected the teacher to ask him to leave. He turned and went outside, and the students almost ran over each other in an attempt to get outside.

Sharon waited until they were all out of the room, and then, slowly, she walked down the aisle, her lips tight and her hands trembling slightly. When she stepped outside, she saw that the students had formed a crowd and Lee was already going into his spiel.

"Lone Wolf made this bow and these arrows himself," he said, lecturing importantly, swelling up with pride. "First we'll use this kind of target."

He took a bottle with a neck no more than two inches wide, carried it to the post thirty feet away, and laid it on its side, the mouth facing Lone Wolf. He then turned and said, "This is the easy part." He stepped slightly to one side, no more that three feet away, and said, "Shoot, Lone Wolf."

Sharon instantly called out, "Lee, move away. You might get hurt."

"Aw, that ain't gonna happen," Lee protested, but at the teacher's insistence he moved several feet away. "Go on!"

Every eye was fixed on Lone Wolf. He held the bow in his left hand, and in a fluid motion he pulled the arrow, notched, and drew it. A gasp went up when the arrow went directly into the mouth of the bottle, knocking it off the post. The students all applauded, and Lone Wolf, despite himself, smiled.

Lee now began what he had worked out the night before and all the way into town with Jason. He set up the targets he had brought with him farther and farther back until Jason was knocking them off at distances that seemed impossible. Finally Lee held up his hand, and after a prolonged burst of applause for a difficult shot, said, "You watch this." He took something that looked like a ball, which was really a horseshoe wrapped in cloth that was tied in a knot, and said, "You ready, Lone Wolf?"

"Ready."

Lee wound up and threw the ball high into the air. When it was exactly at the apex, Sharon saw the tall man pull the bow to full length and loose the arrow. It flew so fast she could barely follow it, but she saw the arrow strike the ball, and it fell to the ground, pierced by the arrow.

Applause went up from all the children, and Lee announced, "Lone Wolf is teaching me to shoot like that."

Sharon said, "Is that all the demonstration, Lee?"

"Well, I guess so. Ain't it keen, Miss Templeton? I bet you never saw anything like that."

His question seemed to bother her, and her eyes glazed over. She tried to ignore it, saying, "All right, come inside."

Lee was disappointed at her reaction and said, "Lone Wolf, why don't you hang around town until after school? Then you can go home with us again, and we can work on that bow you're gonna make me."

Lone Wolf hesitated. "I guess I ought to go back to Slash A," he said. But Lee continued to beg him, and finally he shrugged and said, "All right. I'll be here when you get out."

Lee moved inside reluctantly, and Lone Wolf gathered the arrows and put them into the quiver. Then he noticed that the teacher had remained outside and was watching him. Somewhat baffled, he moved over toward her and stood in front of her. He had not noticed before how small she was. Small but beautiful, even in the plain brown dress that she wore. She made no attempt to flaunt her womanly figure. Lone Wolf felt a slight attraction to her, as much as he had ever felt for any white woman. Feeling the power of her gaze, he said, "Thanks for letting me come. It meant a lot to Lee."

"That's why I did it," she said briefly. Her eyes were fixed on him in a peculiar fashion, which made him feel uncomfortable. Her lips were pressed closely together, and there was a tension in her back. She held herself very straight and finally said, "Thank you on Lee's behalf. I understand from Mr. Reno that you didn't get much chance to learn while you were with . . . your people."

He knew it was not what she had intended to say, but he merely shrugged, saying, "My foster mother was a white woman. She taught me to read and write, but not very well."

"I'll—I'll send some books with Lee that might help you," Sharon said, then turned away and went back in the schoolhouse.

Lone Wolf turned back and walked to his horse, leaped onto its back, and rode away. The scene had seemed strange to him. She had looked at him with such an odd expression that he could not fathom it. All day, from time to time as he roamed the countryside, he wondered but could not understand it.

★ ★ ★

Just as the school let out, Sharon glanced out the window and saw a rider whom she took at first to be Lone Wolf, but then as he came closer she saw that it was Jim Reno.

She dismissed the class but said, "Lee, you remain here. I need to talk with you."

Lee said, "Aw, Miss Templeton, Lone Wolf will be waiting for me."

"You won't be very long. I see Mr. Reno coming. He probably wants to find out about your progress."

Lee plopped back in his seat and fidgeted until Jim entered. Jim pulled off his hat. He was covered with trail dust, and his face was lined with fatigue. "Hello, Miss Templeton," he said.

He would have said more, but Lee jumped up and said, "Jim, did you catch the rustlers?"

"Rustlers?" Miss Templeton said, looking at the man before her with alarm. "I don't understand."

Reno shrugged and said, "I'm surprised you haven't heard. There's a rustler ring operating in this valley. Every stock owner has lost cows, and they hit us two nights ago. I've been out chasing them ever since." He looked over at Lee and said, "No luck, Lee." A faint grin creased his lips, and he shrugged fatalistically. "Rain washed out all the tracks." Then he looked back at the teacher and said, "Just came by on the way home to get a report on this youngster here."

"I'm glad you did," Sharon said quickly. "Come in and sit down. You look thirsty."

"Well, I could use a drink of water."

Sharon indicated the bucket, and he went over and got a dipper and drained it and filled it again. When he had quenched his thirst, she said, "Why don't you sit down, Mr. Reno? I want to talk to you about Lee."

"Jim's good enough, Miss Templeton," he said and took his seat. He sat there while she began speaking, telling him in effect that Lee was a very bright boy. She looked over and said, "I wanted you to hear this, Lee, because you haven't been doing your best, and I wanted you to know, as well as Jim, that you're not living up to your potential."

"Oh, I don't see any sense in it," Lee said. "I mean, I'm not gonna be a teacher. I'd rather be out learning how to work cattle and how to trail things like you, Jim, and like Lone Wolf."

Sharon said instantly, with displeasure, "That's not going to be your career. Handling stock, perhaps, but riding all over with an Indian isn't my idea of a way to live."

Instantly Reno recognized her displeasure with Lone Wolf. He had noticed it before and would have asked about it except for Lee. But he said instead, "What does he need to do? More work at home?"

Sharon was serious about her work. She saw in Lee Morgan one of those rare persons who could be a great student, and she spent some time discussing the possibilities with Reno. Finally she smiled and said, "I don't want to be hard, but I hate to see a mind wasted."

Reno glanced at Lee and said, "That's it, Lee. Get ready to work."

Lee did not complain anymore. Whatever Jim Reno said was law to him. He got up and followed Reno as he left, bidding good-bye to Miss Templeton.

As soon as they stepped outside, Reno's eyes cut to the right, where he saw a group of five horsemen approaching. Reno prepared for action as he saw that it was Jack Bronte and his gang. Faye O'Dell, the tawny hired gunman, was riding beside Bronte, and Burl DeQuincy, whom he had flattened in the brawl, followed, with Paint Clovis and Bat Murdoch. He saw the group spot him, and Faye O'Dell yelled, "There he is. Let's settle it."

"Get out of the way, Lee." He thought of Sharon and hoped that she would stay inside the schoolhouse. Moving away from the building, he was soon facing the men, and Bronte grinned at him.

"Well, Jim, looks like you're all alone this time." Bronte glanced over and said, "Burl there, he feels like you didn't give him a fair shot." Burl DeQuincy came out of the saddle and advanced toward Reno. Clovis and Murdoch got down with him.

Reno knew they intended to rough him up, and he said, "Stay back" as he made a slight move toward his gun.

He had taken his eyes off Faye O'Dell, and he heard the gunman's voice say, "Hold it, Reno." Reno looked up to see that the gunman had drawn on him and was holding the gun steady. "Just get rid of that gun, or I'll take it you mean to use it."

Jim Reno knew death when he saw it, and he saw it in the light green eyes of Faye O'Dell. Reno had a well-developed sense of survival, having learned in the war and through a hard life. He knew what he had to do. Unbuckling his gun belt, he let it drop to the ground and then turned to face DeQuincy, who was coming straight at him. The other two, Clovis and Murdoch, fanned out, both grinning. Reno always believed in a good offense. He stepped forward quickly, before DeQuincy could get his hand up, and threw a left that caught the well-muscled brawler over the eye. DeQuincy let out a yell and countered with a roundhouse swing. He was an awkward, bruising brawler, and Jim could have held his own. But, as he had feared, Clovis and Murdoch suddenly lunged at him, each of them grabbing an arm.

"Bust him up, Burl," Faye O'Dell said. O'Dell was grinning, and he looked over to see that a woman had come out of the school. "You watch this, Teacher," he said. "You'll learn something you won't find in your books. Go on, Burl. Break his back!"

Helplessly, Jim stood there, ducking the first punch that DeQuincy threw, but could not dodge the powerful blow that took him in the side, robbing him of breath. DeQuincy grinned and said, "That'll slow you down" and threw a punch that caught Jim high on the head and turned the world into a spinning wheel of fire.

Sharon stood there, her mouth open in shock, and she cried out but knew that it would do no good. "Leave him alone!"

"Just stand there, Teacher," O'Dell said. "Maybe I'll pay you some attention when we finish up with Reno."

Lee's face was pale, but he moved forward, fists clenched. O'Dell whirled but grinned when he saw the youngster. "Stay out of this, kid!" he warned.

He had no sooner spoken when he heard a hissing sound, and suddenly his hat left his head. Bewildered, he turned his head around and saw that a tall, bronze-faced man had stepped around the corner of the school. He was carrying a longbow, and even in that short space it had taken O'Dell to turn, he had fitted an arrow and now drew it back full length. "Call off those men," he said quietly.

DeQuincy, Clovis, and Murdoch stopped and whirled to look at where O'Dell was staring. "An Injun," Murdoch said. He was an old mountain man and had no fear of death. "Well, lookie here, Jack. We're gonna get us a redskin."

Jason, hearing the man addressed as Jack, knew this was Jack Bronte. He had heard from his father, Reno, and others that this was the leader of the gang that dwelled in the pocket and had been rustling cattle. At once he turned his steel-tipped arrow toward Bronte and said, "Call off your dogs, or I'll put this right in your heart."

Bronte's head flew up, and his eyes blinked in surprise. He saw the tension in that bow and knew that all the man had to do was release it and he would be struck. Shock held him where he was, and he heard O'Dell say, "He's only got one arrow. Gun him down, gun him down."

"Make up your mind, Bronte, if this is a good day to die. One man moves, and your horse loses its rider."

Jack Bronte was a tough man. He had faced more than his share of men across a gun, but there was something in the sight of that steel tip that glinted from the rays of a dying sun. He could almost feel it ramming through his chest. Twice he had seen men struck by arrows in the body, and knew that the only way to get them out was to shove them through, break them off, then withdraw them. Providing, of course, it missed the heart. For one instant, he thought, *I can bluff this Indian.* But then, one look at the light blue eyes that stared at him, and he knew he dare not risk it.

"Do it. Get out of here or take an arrow," Jason commanded.

Bronte said, "All right, boys, get back on your horses."

"Look, we can handle this," DeQuincy said. "Just let us—"

"Do what I tell you," Bronte said. "It's not your chest that arrow's pointed at."

Reno, in the meantime, had gotten to his feet. He picked up his gun belt, removed the .44, and held it loosely in his hand. "Make up your mind, Jack," he said. "You can have it if you want it."

That settled the issue. Bronte said, "Come on." The three moved to their horses and mounted. O'Dell still looked like he had the urge to fight, but the arrow was still pointed straight at Jack Bronte, and Bronte said, "We'll see you later, Jim. Things'll be a little different."

"Get out, Jack. Or pull that fancy gun of yours."

Bronte, however, shook his head and led the group away at a fast gallop.

Reno slowly fastened the gun belt around his middle, buckled it, and then turned to Lone Wolf, who had relaxed the string and was replacing the arrow in the quiver.

Reno studied him then said offhand, "I owe you one for that, Jason. They would have made mincemeat out of me."

Jason took the bow, rubbed his hand up and down the length of it, then said, "That's the man that is stealing the cattle from my father?"

"Probably is. No proof, though."

"But you think it is?"

"I think so."

"I should have killed him."

Reno said instantly, "No. We have to find a legal way."

Jason looked over to where Lee had been standing and from where he was now rushing toward them. He did not want the boy to hear, but he could not help saying, "The Indian way is better."

Reno stared at him, shrugged, and said quietly, "Probably so in this case." He turned to Sharon and saw the shock in her eyes. "Sorry about the fracas."

"Those men—they would have beaten you." Her eyes

went to Lone Wolf, but she said nothing. Then she whirled and entered the schoolhouse.

Lee swallowed, and his eyes were filled with worship as he studied Jason. Reno observed the young man and thought, *To a boy, Jason is quite a fellow.* Then as he studied the bronzed face of the tall man, he had a second thought. *I guess I think so, too. If he hadn't been here, it would have been tough. I wish his dad could have seen it!*

TEN
*Danforth Gets
His Back Up*

Removing the cell key from his battered desk drawer, Lige Benoit moved over to the cluster of three cells, inserted the heavy key, and turned it. The squeaky noise caused the lanky cowboy that lay on the cot to turn his head and stare at the sheriff.

"Come on, Tom. You can go now," the sheriff said, pulling the door back. He watched as the young man, who was sporting a black eye and wearing ripped clothing, located his hat, pulled it onto his head, and stood up.

"I'll get your gun," Benoit said. He walked to a row of pegs, selected a gun belt, and handed it to the young man. "Tom, you're wasting your life like this. Aren't you ever gonna learn to behave yourself?"

A rash grin appeared on the young man's face. He belted on the gun and said, "I must of had a good time last night, Sheriff. I don't remember it, but I couldn't of got hurt this bad without something happening." He shoved his hands into his pockets, brought them out empty, and said, "Busted. Now I'll have to work another two months before I can have another go at the faro table over at the Red Dog."

Benoit shook his head as the young man walked stiffly out, nursing his bruises. Moving over to the window, he looked out on the street and grew thoughtful. The town was the only home he had. He kept himself so rigidly behind a wall that although he was on good terms with the citizens, he had no close friends. The thought disturbed him, which was rare, for he was not given to thinking of his own misfortunes. Moving impatiently from the window, he walked to the rack and pulled on his coat. He jammed his hat on his head and stepped outside.

The late-October air was biting, presaging a winter that would be hard, he thought. Somewhere over the hills that lay to the west, the cold weather waited and one day would sweep over the plain, turning all the grass yellow in a single night. Benoit watched his breath rise in a steamy cloud and then ambled along toward the Rainbow Café.

Stepping inside, he was surprised to see Reverend Allen Danforth and went at once toward him. "Hello, Reverend," he said. He grinned slightly and said, "Can you stand some company this morning?"

"Sit down, Sheriff," Danforth said, a grumpy quality in his voice. "You might be better off somewhere else. I might bite you like I've been snapping at everybody else lately."

Benoit's grin grew broader. He liked the young minister very much and had gone back to church often since the time Lillian had finagled him into attending services. He sat down, and Agnes came over and took his order. She returned moments later, bringing him his own special oversized mug of black coffee, and he smiled at her. "Thank you, Agnes." Then, after she left, he studied Danforth. "Well, I heard about the meeting," he said.

"I guess everybody has." Danforth was staring down at the pancakes on his plate. He'd cut half of them into small bites and had poured some maple syrup over them. Spearing one of the pieces, he shoved it around on the plate, soaking up the sweet syrup, and stuck it in his mouth, chewing violently. "I felt like I'd been to the woodshed after the deacons and elders got through with me!"

The sheriff smiled sheepishly. "Know what you mean. I've had several meetings like that with the town council." He sipped the coffee cautiously, enjoying the scalding warmth as it made its way down his throat. He wanted to speak to the young man as an older man wants to instruct youngsters, but he knew he had to be very careful so as not to offend the man. "You know, there's no such thing as a cup of coffee too big or too hot," he said, and for a while he just sat there, making an idle shape in the chair. He noted the lines of dissatisfaction that marked young Danforth's face. The minister's brown eyes were dark with barely concealed anger, and the shock of curly brown hair was not combed. *He looks like he's been up all night.* Benoit had heard through several sources the story of the meeting when the elders had gotten together and told their pastor he was being too rough with his preaching.

Agnes brought Benoit's order to the table, and the sheriff smiled and nodded his thanks to Agnes. Then looking at Danforth, he said very seriously, "I got a theological question for you, Reverend."

Allen looked up at him quickly. He was interested in the sheriff and wanted to see him find some walk with God, which he appeared not to have. "What is it?" he asked at once.

Benoit said, keeping a straight face, "Well, in a case like this, you already said the blessing over your own grub. Now do you suppose it covers my grub, too? Or do we need to give the calf another lick?"

Danforth laughed abruptly, good humor coming to his face. "You're a butter-fingered scoundrel, Lige Benoit." He speared another three morsels of the pancakes, jammed them into his mouth and, as he chewed, mumbled over them. "I'd say your food is as blessed as most of it gets blessed." He swallowed the pancake, washed it down with a cup of coffee of his own, then began eating the bacon rather hungrily. "I got so mad I didn't eat last night," he said.

"I wish I could've been there. From what I hear, it was quite a yelling match. And since you have the loudest lungs— being a preacher and all—I would assume you won."

"Well, you'd assume wrong, then. They told me they'd had enough of my hard preaching. Kyle Poindexter told me I could either lighten up or get out. He said there are plenty of other preachers to pick from."

"What did you say to that, Reverend?"

"I told him I was looking for a church when I found this one, and I can just go on and find another. Any preacher that only preaches what the congregation wants to hear ain't worth nothing."

"You think they might do it? Run you off, I mean."

"I think they might."

"What did you do that got them so stirred up?"

"Why, you were there, Lige," Danforth said. "It was that sermon where I talked about how people had treated the new Meade boy."

"I remember that." Sitting back, he thought back to that sermon when the minister had raked the congregation, all guns blazing, about the lack of love and response they had shown to Lone Wolf. Ordinarily he was a gentle preacher, gently encouraging and correcting, but Lige remembered how his brown eyes had blazed and he had pounded the pulpit. He said, "I thought you were gonna pull a gun and start cleaning house that morning. You were right, though. We ain't been very hospitable to that young fellow."

"No, and I'm ashamed of the church and ashamed of the town. For two cents I'd pack my suitcase and pull out."

Benoit shook his head. "That wouldn't do no good, Reverend. Wherever you went, you'd find people just like us." He ate slowly, thinking about it. "I think we're afraid of new things, and Jason Meade—Lone Wolf—ain't like nothin' we've ever seen before. People around here still remember fightin' the Indians when we settled Banning. Some of them lost families— husbands, brothers, wives, and kids. That boy is no Indian— and yet he *is* in a way. He looks like one and goes by that Indian name, and everybody knows he's been with the Sioux all of his life. I guess he took part in everything, even the raids. So when folks look at him, that's what they think of."

Danforth bit his lip and worried the morsels of pancakes around on his plate. "I guess so," he said. "But Christians ought to be different. They ought to be willing to open up to people and not prejudge others."

"Well, I'm no Christian, but I've got to admit I haven't been as friendly as I should be. Shoulda gone out there and spent some time with the boy." He started to say more, then he broke off as Lillian Reynolds entered the café. At once he stood up and said, "Over here, Lillian. Join a couple of lonesome bachelors."

Lillian had come into town with Deacon Boone, the cook, to replenish their supplies and had left him at the general store. Being hungry, she had decided to go get breakfast, and she came at once to take the chair that the sheriff pulled out. "I don't want to break into your conversation."

Danforth waited until she was seated, until Agnes had taken her order for bacon and eggs and toast. "Well," he said, "you might as well know. I may not be your pastor much longer." He had tried to keep his anger down, and now the thought of the injustice of it showed in his eyes and in his quick movements.

"Oh, that can't be, Allen!" Lillian felt a motherly instinct toward the young man and longed to see him married off. She had told Mona, "If you weren't already married, I'd see to it you marry that young preacher." She knew instantly it was about the meeting and tried to calm his nerves down.

But he remained adamantly determined to push the matter. Finally he rose and said, "Sheriff, you can pay for my breakfast" and grinned as best he could. "Preachers are prob'ly poorer than sheriffs. I'll see you later." He walked out of the door, his back straight and rigid.

"That young fellow is in a bad way," Lige said. At that moment Agnes came back with a plate of eggs and bacon. She set them down, and Lillian thanked her.

Lige stared at her, and a grin touched his lips. "You don't have to bless the food, Lillian. I straightened that out with the preacher. His blessing covers everything that's set on this table."

"Oh, Lige, what a thing to say!" Lillian laughed. She made an attractive picture as she sat there, the sunlight lighting her brown hair, bringing out the traces of red. She was wearing a rather elaborate dress for a town trip, light blue with dark blue lace trimmings, and her figure was more like that of a girl of twenty than of a woman of forty-five. There was a vivacity to this woman that Lige Benoit felt drawn to. It had become a sort of tradition that after church he and Lillian would spend Sunday afternoon together, either with the family at Sun or in town at the café.

He sat there leaning back, sipping his coffee from time to time. Lillian, obviously worried about the situation at church, spoke of her doubts, and Lige tried his best to assure her. "These things come and they go, they pass. He's young, Lillian, and got to take his knocks the way the rest of us have."

"I suppose so, Lige." She leaned over unexpectedly and put her hand on his arm, a smile drawing her lips up. She had a beautiful complexion, and her lips were full and moist as she said, "Here I am, pouring all my troubles out on you."

Lige Benoit was extremely conscious of the pressure of her hand on his arm, and then he said something that he had not planned to say but that seemed to arise out of his deepest being. "Lillian," he said slowly, putting his eyes on hers. "Have you thought of me as a man you might marry?"

Lillian Reynolds seemed to freeze, her hand still on his arm for a second or two, and then she removed it and looked down at the table. "Why—I never—," she stammered. And then she lifted her eyes and met his eyes fully. "Yes, Lige, I have."

Her words sent a shock through him. He had not expected her to say such a thing, and he swallowed hard. "You know pretty well what I am. Not much dash about me. You'd never know mistreatment from me, and I have to tell you, Lillian, I've got a feeling for you that I've never had for another woman on the face of the earth." He cleared his throat and seemed to find it difficult to speak. "Hard for a man like me to

GILBERT MORRIS

talk of love. I've led a hard life, and you don't know the worst
of it. I never had a family, but, well, what I'm trying to say," he
said, still struggling for words, "is, I love you, Lillian, and I'd
like to spend the rest of my life with you."

"Oh, Lige." Lillian's eyes were misty, and she bit her lip.
"I never dreamed of such a thing—that you'd ask me, and I
can't give you an answer." She saw his face grow tight and said
at once, "For one thing, you're not a Christian. Since I became
a Christian this past spring I've come to see how important it
is that both marriage partners be equal in their spiritual state.
And I know that you wouldn't become a Christian just to please
me. You've got more strength than that."

Lige kept his eyes engaged with hers and said, "Nothing
may ever come of it, but I want you to know one thing, Lillian.
I'm pleased that you'd even think of me in those terms." He
changed the subject, and Lillian knew that he would not speak
of it again until many things changed.

★ ★ ★

The morning wore on, and Allen Danforth made his pastoral
calls, even going by to visit the leader of the faction that was trying to move him out of the church. Kyle Poindexter greeted him
coolly, nodding slightly, and Danforth said at once, "Brother
Poindexter, I know we have differences, but we're both Christians, and I apologize if I was personally offensive to you."

Poindexter opened his eyes wide. He knew the stubborn-
ness of his pastor and said, "Well, that makes a difference,
Preacher." He began to smile and said, "I knew you'd come
around to my way of thinking."

"No. Not that. I still think we've been self-righteous about
Lone Wolf, and he's just part of it. Our church hasn't shown

love for many. We've become a little holy club, meeting in that
box on Sunday and then living like we please the rest of the
time."

"That's just not so, Preacher," Poindexter protested.
"We've done lots of good things, and you've done a lot of good
here, too." Poindexter was a proud man but a fair one, and he
spoke pointedly. "You're just young and want to change everything today. But you don't know what it's like. My folks had to
fight the Indians. My dad carried an arrowhead in his back till
the day he died, and I've seen a little of them red devils myself.
People don't forget that."

"But that's not the same, is it? He's a white man."

Poindexter's eyes narrowed, and he shook his head. "I
don't think he is. Look at the way he dresses—look at the way
he lives. Some of the hands at Slash A told me he has yet to hit
a lick of work. He doesn't care anything about that ranch. All
he does is hunt and fish and loaf. That's the way all Indians
are, and he was with 'em too long."

Danforth listened as Poindexter listed the reasons why
Lone Wolf would never change, and he finally said, "Well, I'm
sorry if I got too rough on a personal level" and then left the
store. He walked down the street slowly, wondering about how to
change people's minds, and finally a thought came to him. He
went to his horse, mounted, and rode out of town. When he got
to the Middleton house, he stepped out of the saddle, tied the
horse, and went up to the front door. Mrs. Middleton met him at
once, and he entered the house and sat down, talking with her
for some time. She was singing the praises of the schoolteacher,
how much she had done for her children, and finally, even as she
spoke, Sharon Templeton came down the steps.

Danforth stood up at once, and he saw a slight flush on

her cheeks as she saw him. He didn't miss the motion that turned her ruined cheek away from him. "Oh, I didn't mean to interrupt," she said.

"Now you just sit right down here, Sharon," Ann Middleton said. "I'm making some muffins in the kitchen, so you two just sit and visit while I go finish them, and then we'll all have them with some tea." She left at once, not giving the woman a chance to protest.

Danforth said at once, "I didn't really come here to see Mrs. Middleton, as enjoyable as that is," he said. "I came here to talk to you."

Instantly Sharon stiffened and said, "Yes, what is it, Reverend?"

"Do we have to stand up?" Danforth asked. "This may take a while."

Sharon took a seat on the horsehair sofa, and he sat down across from her in a rocker. "What is it you want to talk to me about?" she asked, and there was a challenge in her voice. It was as if she was about to be tried, and he saw that she was not open to anything personal.

"I've come to talk to you because you're a leader in the community, and as such you set an example."

"Example?" She was surprised and said, "What do you mean an example? Do you have any complaints about the way I behave myself? I'd be glad to hear them."

"For one, I wish I could persuade you to come to church." He stared at her curiously and said, "Most women of your age are a little more inclined to do such things as that." He waited for a reply, and then he shrugged and moved on to his second concern. "But, that's your own business. What's my business is the way you treat Lone Wolf."

Instantly her lips tightened, and her hands that she held clenched on her lap grew tense. "I don't understand you. What do I have to do with him?"

Danforth leaned forward, speaking clearly, and there was displeasure in his eyes. "I think you know what I'm talking about. I don't know why you have such strong feelings against him, but you've certainly made it plain to everybody in this town." He saw the denial form on her lips, and he shook his head. "Don't bother to deny it. It's obvious every time you look at him, every time he gets near."

"I don't think it's any of your business!"

"This town is my business. You're not in my church. If you were I would have been here long ago. But I want to point out that as a schoolteacher you are looked up to by your pupils. More than one of them have asked me why you hate Lone Wolf. They saw how you treated him when he came to the school and at every occasion since. What am I supposed to tell them? That you hate Indians?"

A strange expression came to Sharon's face, and she rose up at once. "I'm sorry. This is a matter that I refuse to discuss with you." She turned and headed back for the hall.

But Danforth stood up and said, "Oh, I see. You can tell your pupils, then, 'Love your neighbor if his skin is white.'"

But she did not turn and did not speak, her back was straight as she disappeared down the hall, and when Danforth sat down he discovered that his hands were trembling. He was angry beyond measure at the woman.

But if he could have seen Sharon as she mounted the stairs and went into her room, he might not have been so harsh. She shut the door and walked blindly into the room and stood there. Slowly the tension racked her body, and she could not conceal the trembling. She moved over to the bed, sat down and clasped her hands, and for a long time sat there. And then tears began to form in her eyes. She dashed them angrily away and said, "He can't say that to me—he can't!"

But she found no rest and finally did something she had not done for years—she turned and lay face down on the bed and wept. But now her whole body was wracked with sobs, and downstairs on the porch Old Blue, the hound, heard her, lifted his head, and let out a high-pitched whine.

ELEVEN
Incident at Bear Creek

When Sharon entered the general store, she was tempted to turn and leave. The weather was bad enough to keep most people inside, but Kyle Poindexter, the owner, had an audience and was holding court. He turned quickly and said, "Well, come in Miss Templeton. We need some help on this thing."

Sharon nodded at Raymond Sims and Harley Atkins, who were sitting in cane-bottomed chairs hugging the wood-burning stove, which glowed cherry red. They spoke, and she returned their greetings, then said, "I'm afraid I won't have time to talk, Mr. Poindexter. I want to get these things and put them in a cloth sack if you will, please."

Poindexter took the slip of paper she handed him and began hauling items off the shelf. He was, however, a garrulous individual whose tongue was completely disconnected from the rest of his body. Easy had remarked that Kyle Poindexter had a tongue long enough to sit in the living room and lick the skillet in the kitchen. He began at once, picking up where he had left off. "Now, as I was saying, we got to do something about that preacher. He's chasin' around after that wild Indian, and the next thing you know he'll be bringing black people into the church." He slammed a can of peaches down on the table, and his eyes were cloudy with displeasure. "I admire the young fellow for trying some new things, but he's gone too far this time, don't you reckon, Miss Templeton?"

Sharon did not want to become involved with the factions that had developed in the church. Lone Wolf had become a symbol of Reverend Danforth's efforts to change things, but so far she had kept from taking sides. Now she said, "I really don't have the time to talk about it. Is that stick candy I see there? Five sticks of that in with the order, please. And hurry, if you will, Mr. Poindexter."

Poindexter scowled at her but filled the order quickly, tallying the items efficiently and shoving them into a brown cloth sack he produced from beneath the counter. "That'll be four dollars and twenty-nine cents."

Sharon reached into her pocket, pulled forth a small purse, and counted out the amount. When she picked up the sack, Raymond Sims said, "I hope you ain't going out in this weather, Miss." He spat an amber stream of tobacco juice at the stove and admired it as it hissed loudly. Casting a look outside, he nodded his head sagely. "That could be a blizzard shapin' up. You'd best not go far."

"I know something about storms, Mr. Sims." Sharon gathered the sack, turned, and moved toward the door."

"Well, a blizzard ain't no storm," he said. "It's an act of God! Anybody that gets caught in one ain't got no hope. You'd better mind what you're doing—"

But the young woman had made her exit, and Poindexter said sharply, "She may be smart, but she sure ain't easy to get to know, is she?" He quickly forgot her and once again plunged into his nefarious plans to rid the church of Reverend Allen Danforth.

As Sharon left the store and headed for the livery stable, she pulled the brown wool coat more closely about her and shivered slightly. It was only the fifth of November, but the temperature had dropped alarmingly that morning. She was glad now that she'd purchased a pair of fur-lined leather gloves and extra-heavy wool socks. Moving down the street, she wound her way to the livery stable, where Lynn Fogleman came to his feet in surprise when she entered. He too was hugging the stove, and he asked in surprise, "Why, Miss Templeton—?"

"I need to rent a horse, Lynn. Let me have Lady, if you will."

Fogleman stared at her with something akin to shock on his round face. "Why, you can't go out in weather like this, Miss," he protested. "It's fixin' to do somethin' turrible out there!"

"I know it's bad," Sharon said, "but I've got to get out to the Porters. Janie Porter has been sick for a week, and I need to go take some of her work to her." She handed the sack to the rotund stable owner, asking, "Please tie this to the saddle, would you?" She did not answer as Fogleman protested vehemently. Finally he shrugged and went outside. Soon he stepped inside with a bay mare, and Sharon went over to pat the horse's nose while Fogleman put the saddle on. When he was finished, she put her foot in the stirrup and mounted with an ease that delighted her. She had taken riding lessons for several weeks and had found that she had a natural aptitude for it. Nevertheless, Fogleman called out as she turned Lady's head and headed toward the door, which he opened, "You hear that wind whistlin'? You stay on the road, Miss Templeton.

'Cause if you get off of it, you'll get lost—and ain't no way we can find you if a snowstorm comes."

"I'll be all right, Lynn," she called out, and she touched her heels to the mare's side. The horse, eager for the exercise and nervously sensing the ensuing storm, moved at once into a gallop. Sharon pulled lightly on the reins to bring Lady to a smoother pace, and the well-formed bay mare responded by stretching her long legs and lowering her head, moving into the easy, rocking-horse motion Sharon had found to be most comfortable during her riding lessons. Lady was a sturdy quarter horse with a healthy, shiny coat and a long, flowing mane and tail. She seemed to enjoy the stride as much as Sharon did. The whistling wind and approaching storm would have made a younger horse skittish and unruly, but after her first burst of speed the only sign Lady gave of being aware of the weather was the movement of her ears in both directions at the sounds of the wind stirring the countryside.

The sky was a dull, leaden gray, and although it was only a little after one o'clock, already the world seemed to be darkening. As Sharon brought Lady to a trot, she looked up and began to doubt her mission. *Maybe they're right. It wouldn't do to get caught out in a storm.* However, she liked Janie Porter very much and felt some risk was justified. The girl, who was only twelve, had a hard life, living with a dirt-poor family, and was a bright child who had caught Sharon's attention.

Two hours later the sky darkened to a sable hue, and Sharon turned west, heading toward the wooded area. She'd been to the Porters before—a small place on the edge of a scrub-oak forest. They existed by raising a few pigs and a cow and doing a little scratch farming. She suddenly felt something sting her cheek. Startled, she glanced up and saw with alarm that it was beginning to snow. Other tiny flakes began to light on her face, one touching her eye, which caused her to blink. Instantly, she touched the horse with her heels and said, "Come on, Lady—hurry now!" The horse broke into a run, and for the next fifteen minutes, Sharon kept urging her on. The snow did not come as she knew snow to come. There was a howling sound in the air such as she had never heard, like a demented wolf or even a banshee, which she had read about in Gaelic mythology. It howled and screamed faintly and moaned, and the very sound of it seemed to bring a chill to the woman. *I'll have to stay overnight. This snow will be too deep to come back in.* The Porter place was a long ride, over three hours, and she was only a few miles away from the farm. But the snow was now falling in flakes as big as quarters, seeming to strike the ground almost audibly. At first the ground was merely striped with white streaks, but soon the snow built up quickly so that Lady's hooves were muffled and made no sound. There was an eerie quality about that, and the rising wind drove the flakes against her face. They bit her flesh with a cold fire that frightened her.

She was normally not a fearful woman. Her childhood had been unhappy enough and hard enough to teach her not to fear—or at least how to conceal it. Her scarred face had left a mark on her spirit as well. Expecting to be ridiculed as a child, she had learned to harden herself even before the words came. The result was a woman who expected the worst and had learned to brace herself against it. She never once considered that she was attractive. Sometimes she would look at her "good" side and notice the symmetry of her face, but always she would turn—and, seeing the scar, would put another stone in the wall she had built around herself. The scar, strangely enough, had given her strength in a way, as well as weakness—and the strength was now necessary.

The wind rose to a fever pitch, and she urged Lady on. Perhaps she would not have allowed the horse to cross the creek so rapidly if fear had not driven her. During the dry summers Seven Point Creek ran at a mere trickle. But the fall rains had swollen it so that now it spanned at least twenty-five feet. The creek bed also was pitted with deep potholes scoured by the wind. Now as she approached the creek, she saw only that it made a broad black band in the growing darkness with white on both sides. "Come on, Lady!" she cried out, anxious to ford the creek. The mare was confused and tossed her head, giving a slight buck. Sharon kicked her heel into the mare's side and said, "Come on, we've got to hurry!" Lady started across the creek; however, halfway across she stepped into a deep pothole with her left foreleg and went down instantly. Sharon felt the horse going down and had the presence of mind to kick her feet loose of the stirrups, and she tumbled off the horse as it fell. Sharon hit the freezing water face-first—and it was like nothing she had ever felt! She rolled over quickly, afraid that the mare in her efforts to right herself would trample her. As she rolled she forgot to hold her breath, and the freezing water entered her nose, causing her to cough. Water filled her boots, and she finally managed to get on her feet.

Gagging and strangling, she shook her head and looked around to see Lady scrambling up the far side of the bank of the creek. "Lady! Come back!" she called. But the frightened mare did not heed. She bolted and disappeared into the trees. Fear then overcame Sharon, and she thought desperately, *I've got to get out of here!* She did her best to make it to the other bank of the creek, but the water was numbing her feet, and her soaked clothing was stiffening in the cold wind. As she slowly made it across, she wanted to collapse, but she knew that if she did she would never wake up. She moved forward, calling for Lady, hoping that the sound of her voice would bring the mare back. Never had she felt such agonizing cold, and the rising wind screamed with vicious anger as she stumbled forward. The snow was now three or four inches deep and made the footing uncertain. She was not accustomed to walking in riding boots, and hers were now filled with freezing water. Soon she lost track of the path, and she stopped abruptly, the thought running through her like a knife: *I'm lost—I don't see the road!* Wildly she looked around. It was no later than 4:30, but it was as dark as pitch. Fear then took her completely, and she gave in to the panic that had been rising in her. *Lost in a blizzard!* The very words chilled her, and she broke into a stumbling run back in the direction—or so she thought—of where she had crossed the creek. But she was all turned around, and she found herself plowing through a dense thicket with stickers and vines that grabbed at her and tore at her face. She was so frozen that she did not feel the pain.

Finally her breath was gone, and she stood, gasping. Feebly she cried out, "Help, Lady, come back," but her voice was so feeble that she knew that if someone were standing ten feet away, they would not hear it. Part of her gave up then, and yet another part of her urged her on in a desperate attempt to find something that looked familiar, someone who could help. After trudging weakly for another fifteen minutes, she came into a clearing and five minutes later came across the creek. She lurched on and after another five minutes came upon what she believed were the remnants of her footprints from when she had scrambled out of the freezing water. She stared and thought furiously, trying to find the road, but if it was there it was too covered with snow for her to make it out. She fell forward, exhausted, knowing that she was freezing and had no hope of reaching the Porter place.

The sudden onslaught of the blizzard did not disturb Lone Wolf. He had learned how to survive such phenomena years earlier. The stallion he rode was a strong animal, and though they had traveled far that day, Lone Wolf had no indecision about proceeding through the storm until he reached the line cabin that lay four miles ahead. Across the withers of the horse lay a sack full of freshly killed game, including two large rabbits. He carried also his blanket roll, which contained a pistol and several small items of food.

He could not tell exactly where he was with the swirling snow, but the stallion knew enough to keep to the narrow track that formed the road that wound through the heavy woods. Lone Wolf let the horse have his head and thought of nothing except the beauty the snow brought to the woods.

He became alert suddenly when the horse threw his head up and snorted, stepping nervously to one side.

"What is it?" Lone Wolf muttered, and he peered forward. In front of him he saw a dark mass marring the perfect white, and even as he watched, it moved slightly. Instantly he dismounted and approached to investigate. Bending over, he saw that it was a human form, and reaching out he pulled the individual upright. Snow had almost covered the form, and he did not waste time.

"Wake up," he said. He peered into the face before him but could make out only that the eyes were shut and the lips looked white. It was a woman, and he wondered what a lone woman was doing out in a snowstorm. But this was no time for wondering. Quickly he picked her up and carried her to the horse. Slinging her over the animal as he would a slain deer, he leaped astride and held her with his left hand, guiding the stallion with his right. He decided to leave the road and follow Seven Point Creek to the cabin. *It won't be as easy a ride, but it is quicker,* he reasoned. The horse left the trail and walked along the creek's edge, walking in and out of the coursing water. After a couple of minutes Lone Wolf spotted another horse standing by the creek with its tail to the wind. He guessed it belonged to the woman he had rescued, so he rode up to it and tied its reins to his saddle horn and continued on. For twenty minutes Lone Wolf followed the twisting bends of Seven Point Creek. When he came to an enormous tree, he grunted in satisfaction and turned the horse to the right. Five minutes later he slid to the ground and tied the horses to a sapling. He pulled the woman free and carried her over a crest of snow to a small, ramshackle cabin. The door was shut, but he kicked it open and entered. It was pitch dark inside, but he knew the place.

Groping forward, he found a cot and laid the woman down. He quickly turned and went back into the storm. There was a shed in back that had been used for animals, and he led the horses there, tied them carefully, then pulled the game and the blanket roll free and returned to the house. Groping his way along, he was glad to find the makings of a fire. He had left it there himself on his last visit but had expected someone to have used it by now. He built some small twigs into a pyramid and, unfolding his blanket, pulled out a box of matches. He struck one, and it flared in the darkness. He touched it to the twigs, and they began to crackle as a small blaze spread. Slowly, he added larger twigs until finally the cheerful light of the fire illuminated his face. When he had put on several logs half as large as his arm and the fire was going well, he turned to the woman.

She was lying flat on her back where he had left her, and her clothes were frozen stiff and were colored a frosty white. Bending over, he shook her and said, "Wake up! You can't sleep." He watched intently, and her head turned to one side. He looked at the frozen face and saw that her eyelids were iced shut so that she could not open her eyes. He tried to clean them with his hands, and she moaned faintly and tried to move away. He then removed her boots and wet clothing and wrapped her in a wool blanket. Then he lifted the cot with her in it and moved it closer to the fire. Once she was in position, he arranged an ancient table in front of the fire and draped her clothes over it to dry. When that was done, he went back, pulled a cracker box up beside the bunk, and sat down to watch her. His face was impassive, but he recognized that this was Sharon Templeton. Strange thoughts ran through the mind of Lone Wolf, and he sat there immobile, from time to time brushing her face and from time to time getting up to turn her clothes over to dry better. He was adding fuel to the fire when he heard a small sound, and he turned to see that she had awakened and was watching him. At once he moved back to the fire.

Sharon had come out of unconsciousness groggy and dis-oriented. She had only memories of fighting the blinding, freezing snow, and now as she stared at the tall figure in front of her, her mind refused to function. His back was to the fire, and she felt the roughness of the blanket on her body. "Who—

where am I?" she gasped. Her voice sounded feeble and weak, and she tried to sit up.

"Line cabin," Lone Wolf said. He reached over and pushed her back down, forcing her to lie still.

Fear ran through Sharon, but she realized that she was helpless in a strange place, and she lay there trying to speak. Finally she said, "I got . . . caught in the storm."

"You were freezing to death when I found you." As Lone Wolf spoke, he turned his head enough so that the light from the blazing fire fell on his face. Sharon gasped, for she recognized him, but she said nothing. He turned back and said, "How do you feel?"

Sharon shook her head. Her hair was dry now, and she could not have known he had dried it with a piece of sacking he carried in his bedroll. She swayed slightly on the cot and grasped the blanket that lapped loosely over her shoulders. Looking over, she saw her clothes hanging in front of the fire, and her mind went blank for a moment. She looked wildly around the room, but there was no one there except them, and she said, "How did we get here?"

"This is an old line cabin. Used to be used by Slash A, but not enough pasture anymore, I guess. Do you think you can stand up and move around?" When she nodded and tried to get up, he saw how she faltered and reached out and pulled her as he would a child.

Keeping her grasp tight on the blanket, she said, "I'm-I'm all right, just a little weak."

"I'll cook something," he said, and he turned toward the fire. She watched, standing there shakily, and found that she had feeling back in her limbs. She remembered going completely numb so that when she had struck her hands together to try to warm them, she had felt nothing. Now, they were burning, she found, as were her feet. She watched as he took a stick and impaled a portion of the carcass of a rabbit with it, put it over the fire, and then went outside carrying a bucket. He came back with a bucket full of snow and began to melt it. As he knelt down, she asked timidly, "Are my clothes dry?"

"I guess so." He appeared to have forgotten her, keeping his eyes fixed on the snow as it melted and on the rabbit as it began to cook. Sharon had never been in such a position, but she felt paralyzed and helpless with only the blanket around her. Moving feebly, she advanced toward the table, pulled her riding dress off, and found that it was warm to the touch and dry. Quickly she moved back into the shadows and, with one agonizing glance at the man staring at the fire, threw the blanket off and slipped into the riding outfit. The underclothing she still wore was a little damp, but such was her relief to be clothed again that she paid no attention to that.

A few minutes later he turned to her for the first time, and she saw the brightness of his blue eyes as he studied her. "You're hungry," he announced, nodding slightly. "Always that way after you nearly freeze." He pulled the stick back, pulled the carcass of the rabbit off, and began to slice it up. He handed her a quarter of it, and she took it, juggling it because it was so hot. She was, she realized, ravenous, and was prevented only by the scorching heat of the meat from eating it like a hungry wolf. She looked up as she nibbled at it and saw that he was studying her with a peculiar expression. His gaze troubled her, and she dropped her eyes.

"What were you doing out in the storm?" he asked. He cut another quarter off and began cautiously tearing at the meat.

"I set out to go to the Porters, but my horse threw me right into the creek."

"Bad place to get thrown," he said. He was silent then, and the two of them sat there quietly eating.

Finally she said, "This is the best meat I've ever had." He shrugged, saying nothing, and handed her some water in a cup that was chipped around the edge. She washed some of the tough meat down, then continued to eat hungrily.

Finally he said, "Do you want some coffee?" When she nodded, he pulled off a coffeepot that had been bubbling on the back of the coals. He found a tin cup, filled it, and handed it to her.

"Won't you have some, too?"

"Only one cup," he said. "When you finish, I'll have some."

She was embarrassed by that but found the scalding coffee good. When she had drunk half of it, she said, "Now you."

He raised one eyebrow at her, then shrugged his shoulders, took it, and drank several swallows. He filled it up again from the pot and handed it to her.

A thought came to him, and a smile turned the corners of his lips up. "Reminds me of what the missionaries call communion. They passed a cup around, everybody drank out of it."

The fire cracked cheerfully in the fireplace, and after Sharon had eaten and drunk, she felt sleepy. But when her eyes started to close, he said sharply, "Don't go to sleep."

She knew he was warning her about the dangers of freezing, but although that was over, she obeyed his injunction. She was sitting there soaking up the warmth when he asked her suddenly, "Why do you hate Indians?" He stared at her, and there was no anger in his voice, only curiosity.

"Why, I don't hate—" Sharon started to give the polite

denial, but she remembered if it were not for this man, she would be dead. She closed her lips for a moment and looked down at her hands and then lifted her eyes. She turned her face to the side and touched her scar. "Because of this," she whispered.

"An Indian did that?"

"Yes. I was very young, and there was an Indian raid. My father was killed, and I got this. I can still remember it." She stared at him and said, "I have bad dreams about it even now."

Lone Wolf stared at her and understanding came into his eyes. He had felt a strong animosity toward the young woman, but now her statement caught his interest. He knew that Indians learned to hate the whites who killed and butchered their families. He himself had some of this in him, even though he was white. Now, looking at her he knew that for a woman that scar would be a terrible thing, and he also knew how memories sometimes haunted one long after the event. He stared at her for so long that she became nervous. "I've never talked to anybody about it, not in a long time."

"If you were a man, it would not be so bad. A scar can be a badge of courage, a mark of a warrior. But a woman wants to look beautiful," he said simply.

Startled at his perception, she nodded. "Yes," she said in surprise, "I suppose that's true. It's changed everything for me. Other women will marry, have families. I'll never have that now, but I'll have the children I teach."

"That's foolish." Lone Wolf shook his head. "You are a fine-looking woman." She shook her head in protest and touched the scar. "That is nothing," he said. "A man would pay no attention to that if he cared for you."

Sharon sat there in shocked amazement. She had never

spoken to anyone like this, she had never known a man like this. She realized that his years with the Indians had given him a different outlook. She hadn't been truthful enough in what she had said. Magnifying her disfigurement in her own head, she had put marriage and romance out of her head when she was very young, no more than twelve or thirteen, when boys had made fun of her or turned from her in disgust. Now she stared at the bronzed face of the big man in front of her and could not find a thing to say.

"You're afraid of Indians. I knew that all the time. And now I understand why." He saw her nod slightly and said quietly, "Are you afraid now?"

Sharon discovered to her surprise that she was not afraid. The experience had been so terrible and the fear so great that she had not had time or inclination to be afraid. She looked at him and said simply, "No, I'm not afraid."

"I might harm you?" he suggested, watching her carefully.

"I don't think so. If you were going to harm me, you would have done it before now."

A smile touched Lone Wolf's lips, and he leaned back, saying nothing. He sat there in silence and finally said, "I think it'll be all right if you slept some now."

She smiled at him and arose. She was frightfully sleepy and went at once to the bed, wrapped up in the blanket, and lay down. Sleep came to her quickly, but before it did, she looked at him as he sat in front of the fire and said, "Lone Wolf."

He looked over at her, surprise in his face. "Yes?"

"I—I'd like to help you with your reading and writing."

"Maybe." He looked back into the fire.

As she fell back, a warm darkness swallowed her up.

TWELVE
Reno Loses His Temper

Simon Meade sat hunched over in his chair, staring out the window at the white expanse of snow. Here and there he could see the winter grass poking through, for three days after the storm the ranchers had welcomed a warm spell. Meade looked down at his legs, and his jaw tightened. He put his hands on his thighs, squeezed, and then nodded approvingly. Wheeling the chair around, he locked the wheels and grasped the arms until his knuckles turned white. Taking a deep breath, he heaved himself into a standing position, and instantly the room seemed to revolve. He forced himself to keep his eyes open, and finally the motion ceased. Tentatively he took a step forward, teetered dangerously, and then took another. His worn slippers made a sibilant noise as he crossed the room, and when he got to the far wall, he fell against it, keeping himself upright. Finally, gritting his teeth, he turned and started back, his legs trembling with fatigue at the unaccustomed exercise. Five feet away from the chair his right leg gave way, and he fell headlong. He reached out to grab a small table, and he fell on it with a crash, breaking the vase that was on top into smithereens. He lay there rolling helplessly, trying to get up.

"Dad, what in the world—?" Mona had been just in the next room and came rushing to his side. "What were you trying to do?"

Simon Meade rolled over and got up on his knees. The fall had hurt him, but there was a light in his eyes. "I'm trying to get up and walk like a man!" he grated. "Just had a little fall is all."

"You get right back in that wheelchair!" Mona scolded him, then she pulled at him.

Instead of the wheelchair, he struggled into a cane-bottomed chair and said, "Mona, get my britches."

She stared at him, and then a smile spread across her lips. "You must be getting better, Dad," she said. And then she urged him, "All right, you sit down for a while now, and I'll go get your pants."

Ten minutes later, Simon was sitting in his overstuffed chair that faced the big window. He was wearing his pants and shirt instead of the ratty old robe that had been his garb for many weeks. He looked up as Mona came in and smiled at him. "Got your own way, didn't you?"

Simon reached up and captured her hand. It felt very small under his, and he pulled her around to look up into her face. "I'm glad you came here, Mona. You can't know how much difference it's made, your marrying Lew and coming on the ranch. It's made an old man very happy."

Mona blinked, for Simon Meade did not normally show his emotions, and there was emotion written across his craggy features. Swiftly she scooped down, kissed his cheek, and hugged him for a moment. Then she straightened up and said brusquely, "Now that we've got that out of the way, we can get on. What do you want for supper?"

"A steak," he said. He looked out of the window and shook his head. "We lost cattle, Lew tells me. Always happens with a storm like that one." He pounded the side of his leather chair with his hand and shook his head. "Feel like a baby, tied up here in this chair, but—"

"Don't you worry," Mona interrupted. "You'll be out punchin' cattle again before you know it. Now you sit there, and if you want to walk, you call out. I want to be there to make sure you don't hurt yourself in case you have another 'little fall.' You hear me?"

"All right, I will."

Simon sat there for over an hour, enjoying the feel of the trousers and feeling better than he had in weeks. He was still weak, and there was pain when he twisted his body. He knew that the bullet that had struck him would always give him problems. Nevertheless, he was happy. Looking up, he saw Lew and Charlie Cole ride into view, coming out of the open space to the left. They came directly to the house, dismounted, and came inside.

Lew stopped still and stared at his father and said, "You got your britches on, Dad." A smile spread over his face, and he said, "How'd you get Mona to give 'em to you?"

Simon returned the smile. "I told her you'd take a stick to her if she didn't mind me and show a little respect for her elders."

Lew laughed and went over and slapped his father on the shoulder. "She knows I'd never do that." He held onto the shoulder and squeezed it. "Good to see you making progress, Dad. He looks good, don't he, Charlie?"

Charlie Cole, the foreman, at the age of forty-three was no more than medium height, slim, lean, and tan from a lifetime of punching cattle under the hot skies. He had hazel eyes and fair hair. "Good to see you up, Mr. Meade," he said.

Simon was accustomed to Cole's lack of wordiness, but he knew that he was a solid man for Slash A. He had been with the ranch for many years but only recently had become foreman when Meade had fired Bax LaFarge for stirring up the range war that had torn up the valley a year ago. "Thanks, Charlie," he said. He looked at the two men and said, "What's the verdict? Did we lose many?"

"No," Lew said, shaking his head. "It wasn't as bad as I thought. Not over five or six that I could find. Course, some of them are pretty far out, scattered, but it doesn't look too bad."

"That's good, Son," Simon said, relieved. Then he said, "You two look froze solid. Help me out of this chair. We're going in the kitchen and sit down while that good-looking wife of yours feeds us something."

Lew stepped over and gave his father a boost out of the chair, and they made their way slowly across, Simon hanging onto the firm frame of Lew. Lew thought, *I never thought I'd see the day when he'd have to hold onto me for help.* But he said nothing about that. When they entered the kitchen and Mona looked up in surprise, he said, "You aim to starve us to death, woman? Get that grub on the table."

Mona made a face at him. "All you ever think about is food."

Lew said earnestly, "No, I think about—something else once in a while."

Charlie Cole laughed out loud, and a smile creased Simon's face. They sat down at the table, and as they drank coffee and waited for the meal, they spoke of the affairs of the ranch. It was Charlie who brought up a subject that had been on his mind. "Mr. Meade," he said, "we don't have enough hands. The boys are about worked to death." He took a sip of the black coffee and then said, "I don't know as it's my place to mention this. I guess it ain't, but I'll say it anyway. We could use your son right now. I don't guess he knows much about cattle, but he's a good rider, and he could track 'em for us."

"He's not here," Simon said briefly.

Cole opened his mouth to say something, his face showing anger, but he closed it again and said, "Well, it ain't my say."

Lew looked over at his father and said, "I'll have a talk with him."

"No. Let me do it," Simon said. "What do you hear about the other ranchers?"

He changed the subject abruptly, and soon they were sitting down to their meal, but Simon Meade had not forgotten Cole's question, and he continued to think about how he could talk to Lone Wolf.

He got his chance, but not until the next afternoon. He watched all day, hoping to catch a glimpse of his son, and Mona was aware that he was moody. He walked a bit more steadily, but it was still quite an effort for him to stand for more than a few minutes at a time. He spent most of the time resting in the overstuffed chair. Finally at 3:15 he looked out and saw Lone Wolf coming, riding his stallion into the yard. Simon was wrestling with the problem of how to talk to him and watched as his son pulled a carcass of a deer off the back of his horse and carried it around to the back. He would, Simon knew, come into kitchen and talk to Mona, and when he heard the door slam, he called out, "Lone Wolf, come in here, will you?"

At once Lone Wolf came to the door. He was wearing denim pants and a buckskin shirt—with no coat even though it was the second week of November—and his face was less coppery than it had been when he had arrived. "Yes, what is it?" he asked.

"Sit down, please." Simon waited till the young man took his seat, then slapped his leg and said, "I'm wearing pants now. Been able to walk a little bit even."

"That's good." There was a watchful air about Lone Wolf, and Simon knew this son of his still did not feel comfortable with him.

He said, "I haven't seen you since you saved that schoolteacher's life. Everybody in the valley's talking about it." When Lone Wolf only shrugged, Simon leaned forward and said, "I wish you had come and told me about it. I like to hear about things like that, especially about you, Son."

"It wasn't that much."

Simon frowned and said, "Well, I think it was, and I'm sure Miss Templeton thinks it was." He hesitated and knew there was no way he could say what was on his mind except in a straightforward way. He took at deep breath and began. "Jason," he said, intentionally using his son's given name, "I've thanked God many times since you've come home for restoring you. But I've got to talk straight to you now." He saw the eyes open up, his son grow cautious. He continued nonetheless. "You've been here for a few months now, and you've had some time to get used to the way things work in a white society. I think it's time that you became part of this family. And I think it's time that you took a hand with the ranch."

"I don't know much about ranching," Lone Wolf said indifferently.

"You're not too old to learn." Simon's voice was sharp, and he forced himself to speak calmly. "Look at it this way, Jason. It's going to be half yours one day, yours and Lew's."

"I don't want a ranch. I wouldn't know what to do with it."

"Confound it—wake up! You can't go back and live with the Indians. You know as well as I do that time is gone, so be sensible." Simon realized he sounded harsh, so he paused and softened his voice. "I know it's been hard on you, and I know people haven't treated you well. But you've got to make some concessions, too."

"Concessions? What do you mean?"

Simon hesitated and then shrugged. "Well, for one thing, cut that braid of yours off. Start using your birth name. Dress like a white man and go to work; make something of yourself."

Lone Wolf grinned thinly. "I thought I was something."

"You know what I mean," Simon said. For the next five minutes he talked as earnestly as he could, trying to be gentle, but he saw that his son's mind was set. The speech was interrupted when he looked up and said, "There comes Reno and a couple of his hands. They've probably come over to offer to help us, but they've got troubles of their own." He hesitated and said, "I'd like to know I can count on you, Son."

Lone Wolf felt strange. He had not spent much time with Simon Meade, his father. He'd felt tremendously uncomfortable around him. The last thing he could think of was showing any emotion toward this man he hardly knew. Steadfastly now, he resisted the temptation that came to him to agree, and he shook his head as he got to his feet. "You spoke of me changing, but you never said anything about others changing to adjust to my ways. Just like white men. I don't need a ranch, and I don't want to fit into a society that won't accept me the way I am," he said. "Is there anything else?" He waited till Simon shook his head, walked through the kitchen straight outside, and began dressing the deer.

A knock sounded and Simon said, "Come in." The door opened and Jim Reno entered.

"Hello, Simon," he said, taking off his hat and coming to stand before the older man. He immediately noticed the improvement in the man since the last time they had spoken. "You're wearing britches! Glad to see you're up to it."

"Thank you, Jim. I'm walking pretty good, too. A little bit more every day."

"That's mighty good news." Reno's tone was sincere, and Simon thought how strange it was that this man that he had hated only a short time ago was more concerned about his well-being than his own son was. "We've about got our cattle all accounted for, so I brought Easy and Leo because I know you've got a lot of ground to cover. If you can put us up, we can spend a couple of days over here."

"You don't have to do that, Jim. But I admit we could use the help. Lew and Charlie were just talking about finding some help. Of course, we'll be glad to pay you."

Reno shook his head. "No, you'll prob'ly have to help us someday, so we'll call it even." He sat down, and as the two sat there talking, Simon found himself telling Reno about the problem with his son. When he was through, he spread his hands apart in a helpless gesture. "I don't know what to do about him, Jim. It's just like talking to a stump. He doesn't listen to anything I say."

"He listens, all right," Reno said. He was dead tired from

a week of hard riding, and the sight of the old man sitting there helpless while the tall son of his did nothing but ride around the country disturbed him. "He's a hero right now for saving Miss Templeton's life, but I gotta tell you, I think it's a shame the way he's failed you."

"Well, it's his bringin' up," Meade said. "Indians don't know much about steady work, do they?"

"No, they don't. They don't really need to. But he's not an Indian now. It's time he faced up to that." Reno found himself getting angry. He had risked a great deal to bring Simon's youngest son out of the Indian camp and to get him back to his own people, and he felt pleased at his success. But now it seemed all for nothing. "Well, there's still time for him to change. Maybe I can have a talk with him. Sometimes outsiders can do things family can't."

"I'd appreciate that, Jim."

Reno got up and left, and when he got to the bunkhouse, he looked around. "Where's Easy and Lee?"

Zero Pounders looked up and said with distaste, "They went over to watch that Injun skin a deer. I wish he'd spend some of that energy helpin' us run these cattle down."

All the crew suddenly saw Reno stiffen. A strange light touched his eyes, and his lips grew into a thin line. Without a word, he whirled and left the room.

"Uh-oh! That looks like trouble," Baldy Sims said. "Wonder what's got Jim's back up?"

Reno walked swiftly to the house, turned, and walked around the corner and found Easy standing off to one side and Lee getting a lesson from Lone Wolf on skinning a deer. Lone Wolf looked up but did not speak as Reno came up.

"Lee, get to the bunkhouse. Easy, you go with him."

Lee stared at him with astonishment. "What's wrong, Jim?"

"I'm gonna have a private talk with your friend here."

Lone Wolf put down the knife, and he turned to face Reno. He was as careful as a man could be, for he knew trouble when he saw it, and he saw it in the tense form of Jim Reno. "What's the matter?" he asked quietly.

Jim tried to keep a hold on his temper, but he did not succeed. He looked over and said, "You heard me, Lee. Easy, take him out of here."

Easy moved forward and said quietly, "Let's go, Lee."

"But—," Lee started to protest.

"You can stay if you want to, Lee," Lone Wolf said. "I don't care if you hear what he has to say."

Reno said, "All right, let him hear it, then." He paused and said, "You're a no-good bum. I thought you'd amount to something if you had a chance, but I see I was wrong. Here your dad's whole ranch is falling down, and all you can do is run around and play Indian. I think you enjoy it when people talk about you, how you're different and all. And I think you're afraid to make the effort to be half the man your father or brother is."

Lone Wolf stepped forward in anger. "I don't have to listen to that!"

"No, you don't have to listen to it. You can get on your horse and ride out and go hunting. But you don't even have your own horse, do you?" Jim's words were hard, and he realized he was making a mistake. He would have turned to go, but he had no chance, for Lone Wolf grabbed him by the front of the coat. Young Meade's eyes were blazing.

"Shut up!" he said. "You think because you helped me a little that you can tell me what to do."

Reno knocked his hand away with his left hand and gave him a shove with his right. "Keep your hands off me," he said, "or I'll break your back."

Perhaps it was because Lone Wolf knew that Reno was right—and that his father was right as well. Everyone had been trying to be gentle and to tell him what to do. All the time he was acutely conscious that he had to make a choice. But Reno's harsh words and blazing anger suddenly shoved him over the edge, and with a wild cry he launched himself at Reno and caught him in the head with a blow that drove Reno to the ground.

Reno hit the ground but kicked out, rolled over, and was quickly on his feet. Stripping off his gun belt, he tossed it aside along with his hat. Then, said, "All right. If you're gonna act like a baby, I'll treat you like one. You need a whippin', and I'm gonna see that you get it."

"Do it, then!"

Lee cried out, "Don't fight—please—"

Easy grabbed the boy's arm and said, "Too late, boy. It's got to happen now." His own eyes were half shut as he watched the two as they came together.

Meade outweighed Reno by twenty pounds and towered over him. The muscles beneath his shirt were large, and when he swung it was with power. But hitting Jim Reno was like trying to hit the breeze. Reno's reflexes were quicker than any man Lone Wolf had ever seen. For as he swung, Reno simply moved his head, and when Lone Wolf fell off balance with the blow, Reno swiveled and threw a hard right that caught the larger man in the side, the pain making him wince. In shame he whirled around, ignored the pain, and lurched again at Reno.

Reno was not aware that the crew had come to watch. He

moved on his feet lightly as Lone Wolf came in throwing thundering blows, any one of which might have ended the fight had they landed.

Reno threw a light left that caught Lone Wolf in the mouth, and blood trickled down his chin. But the blow only infuriated him, and with a quick motion he threw himself at Reno, his arms widespread. He took several blows in the face but managed to grab Reno and throw him to the ground. It was like trying to hold a wildcat down, but with his superior weight he finally managed to wind up on top. He raised his hand and drove a blow into Reno's jaw.

Reno felt the power of the blow, and light exploded before his eyes. He knew that if he did not get up, he would be beaten to a pulp. With a quick wrench of his body he twisted, and throwing Lone Wolf off balance to the right, suddenly twisted to the left and with a lunge was on his feet. Reno waited for his combatant, who got up quickly, and the two circled each other warily.

"That Injun's got more than he could bite off and handle," Baldy said quietly.

"I don't know," Charlie said. "He's awful big and strong as a bull."

That reference to a bull made Easy think of a bullfight he had seen once in Mexico City. A huge bull drove straight at a slim figure that simply turned a fraction of an inch, allowing the needle-sharp horns to go by. And now he saw something of that spectacle in the fight before him. The bull-like Lone Wolf charged Reno, who quickly moved and counterpunched. The two had battled on for a few minutes and were slowing down. And both were considerably bloodied.

They both were arm weary and staggering and would have gone on until both of them were beaten to a pulp, but there was a sudden shout. "Stop it! Stop it right now!" Both men halted wearily and turned to look to where Simon Meade was standing on the porch, leaning against the rail. "Jim, you can't change him like that. He's what he is. Nothing will make him any different. Lone Wolf, you're my son. This is your home as long as you want. You won't be asked to do anything you don't want to. When—or if—you change your mind, we'll be here."

Lone Wolf stared at his father for a very long moment, then turned and walked away. They all watched as he untied his horse from a tree nearby, mounted, and rode away.

Jim looked at Simon and shook his head. "I shouldn't of done that, Simon. I was a fool."

"You did what you thought was right." He turned and walked into the house, helped by Mona, whose face was marked with anguish.

Jim turned and got one glimpse of Lee. The young man's face was etched with pain and doubt and something else. Jim then realized how close Lee had gotten to Lone Wolf and knew that he had thrown the boy into a state of anguish. He moved to Lee, shrugged, and said, "It happens, Lee. Don't let it get to you." But he saw that the young man could not take it that easy, so he shrugged and went toward the bunkhouse.

Easy watched him go, then approached the boy and said, "Lee, that's pretty tough to see. You like both of them, don't you? But that's the way things happen."

Lee looked at him, shook his head, turned abruptly, and walked away. Away from the bunkhouse and away from Jim Reno.

"Here comes Lige Benoit." Chris had come in from the front porch and found his mother sewing. His face showed fatigue from the work of cleaning up after the storm, but a grin touched it now. "I'll get away and leave you two young folks alone," he said slyly.

"Oh, don't be ridiculous!" Lillian said sharply. She got to her feet, and when Chris only laughed at her and went into the kitchen, she quickly went to a mirror and touched her hair up. She didn't wait for the knock but opened the door and found Lige with his fist raised. "Come in, Lige," she said, and she stepped back.

Benoit stepped inside, taking off his hat, and said, "Crew all out huntin' cattle?"

"All except Chris," she said. "He just came in a little while ago. Jim took Easy and Lee over to help at Slash A."

"Guess they can use the help. All the ranchers have been helping each other out."

"Come in, sit down. I've got coffee on. I'll bring it out here."

Benoit smiled and said, "That would be good." He sat down, and soon Lillian was back with the tray. The two sugared their coffee and sat there chatting amiably. Benoit listened to the story that she had to tell him about the fight between Jim Reno and young Meade.

"That fellow's gonna have to get hurt before he's any good," Benoit said. He thought back on his own life and said, "It would have been good for me if I'd a had somebody to beat some sense into me when I was his age."

"That would have been pretty hard, wouldn't it, Lige? You're a stubborn man."

Lige put the cup down and got up and stood over her. Reaching down, he pulled her to her feet and said, "I'm glad you recognize that, Lillian."

"Recognize what?" she asked in bewilderment.

"That I'm a stubborn man." A smile touched his lips, and he said, "I've warned you about what I had on my mind, and I said I wouldn't mention it again until things changed."

Her lips opened with surprise, and then understanding came to her and a flush touched her cheeks. "Oh, Lige! That's wonderful! When did it happen?"

Benoit shifted his feet awkwardly. He hadn't told anyone yet about his becoming a Christian, and he didn't really know how to describe it. But he tried anyway. "It was during the storm. I stopped over at the church to check on the pastor just as it hit hard. We talked while I waited to see if it was going to die down so I didn't have to walk home in a blizzard. We started out talking about his troubles with the elders, and the next thing I knew I was on my knees asking Jesus into my heart." The sheriff paused and shook his head. "I didn't realize how I was carrying my past around like I was. It feels like an anvil's been lifted off my back. Lillian, I wasn't a good man when I was younger, and I did a lot of things that I don't ever want to think about again. I never forgave myself, and I built a wall around myself and wouldn't let anyone in—even as long as I've been in Banning I haven't gotten close to anyone. But now that Jesus has forgiven me, I feel free. I feel I can move on and put the past behind me—where it belongs."

Now he braced himself for what he was about to say. "I can only say what's on my heart. When I asked you to marry me before, you said you couldn't because I wasn't a Christian. I understood your convictions. But now I'm a Christian. So now I'm asking you again. Lillian, will you marry me?"

Lillian paused, her heart beating fast. She had been very happy in her first marriage, but that was a lifetime ago, back in the city when she and Martin had lived affluent lives. Since she'd come west, there had been a loneliness, especially since Mona had married. She had felt the strength of Lige Benoit from the first, and she knew she had to give him an honest answer.

"Lige, I—I do feel something for you. I don't know if it's love, and at our age it's hard to tell, isn't it?"

"I don't know how old you are," he said quietly. "But at my age, I can tell you right now, I'm in love with you, and I think you feel something for me."

"I do, Lige, but—" Lillian pulled her hand away from his, turned, and stepped back. She touched her hair nervously and dropped her hands. "Lige, I'm so glad you gave your life to Christ. It was the best decision you could ever make, and I know you did it for your own good, not just to get me to agree to marry you. But I must tell you . . . ," she said almost breathlessly. Emotions had stirred through her, and she had to force herself to speak above a whisper. "I don't know if I could ever marry a law officer, Lige. I don't think I could stand the thought of someone coming to tell me that my husband had been killed. I've lost one husband already, and I really don't want to go through it again."

Lige stared at her and then nodded. "I understand that, but that could happen no matter who you marry. Even a rancher can get killed by a river or by a wild steer."

"It's not the same, Lige, and you know it. They can try to avoid trouble. You have to confront it."

Benoit conceded her point with a shrug. "I know you're right. It's not right for a woman." He hesitated, then said, "It's not much for a man either, but it's all I know to do right now."

Lillian's lips were tremulous as she smiled and said, "I do

care for you, Lige, but I can't marry you right now. I'm going to need some time to think about it."

"Let me say one last thing, Lillian. I understand you're worried about losing another person you care about. But never taking a chance could be even worse, wondering about how happy you could have been in the time you had together." Benoit stayed only briefly after that, wanting to give Lillian some time to think about what he had said.

After he left, Chris came out of the kitchen, took one look at his mother, and knew something was troubling her. "Did he ask you to marry him?" he inquired.

"Yes, he did."

Chris came to stand beside her. He put his arm around her and, looking down at her, said, "I think you ought to do it. I've seen for quite a while that you care for him."

"I told him I didn't think I could ever marry a law officer. It's no life for a woman, Chris."

Chris shook his head. "I don't know much about things like this, but if you love someone, I guess you take them as they are. At least that's what I think, Mother."

Lillian listened to him carefully, then reached up and patted his cheek. "You're a good boy, Chris. You shouldn't have to worry about your mother's problems."

He leaned down and kissed her cheek. "You're no problem. You're just a woman who needs companionship."

He hugged her and then left the room. Lillian stood watching the door, thinking of Lige Benoit.

THIRTEEN
The Big Steal

Jack Bronte stood on the front porch of his ranch house, staring up at the sky. Even in repose, there was something cruel and dangerous about the man. His eyes were half hooded, and he seemed to be totally idle, yet Faye O'Dell knew him too well to think that he was off guard. "What's up, Jack?" he demanded.

Bronte turned his head and studied O'Dell, who for once in his life was without a gun. The two men had come out after breakfast, and now Bronte said, "I think it's about time, Faye."

At once O'Dell straightened up. He stared into the sky and shook his head. "I don't know. I don't know weather."

Bronte turned his face back, scanned the horizon, and seemed to sniff the air. "We're going to have a big snow. I feel it in my bones. I don't know how I do it, Faye, but I can always foretell the weather. That last storm we had was pretty bad. This one may not be as bad, but there's plenty of snow rolling in, I can tell."

O'Dell stared at him and shrugged. "What's the play?"

"We get all ready. As soon as it starts snowing, we send

the boys out, everybody. This time we'll gather small bunches from each of the ranches, and then we'll put 'em together into a herd."

"Pretty risky, Jack. Spreadin' ourselves thin like that."

"I don't think so." Bronte shrugged. "They'll lay in their bunkhouses waitin' for the snow to quit, and by the time they head back out, we'll have a big herd out of their reach."

"All right," O'Dell said. "But the timing's gotta be right. You let me know, and I'll send a wire to Blandings. He'll have the stock car whenever we say over at Giddings." He shook his head doubtfully. "Everything'll have to be just right."

Bronte looked like a sleek wolf as he turned his head and faced his lieutenant. "It will. I've been waitin' for this one for a long time. What we'll do, Faye, is sell the cattle, lay the boys off, and lay low for a while. We'll have plenty of money, maybe take a trip down to old Mexico and live like kings, just me and you."

"What about the boys?"

Bronte shrugged and said nothing, and a small, cruel smile played around O'Dell's lips. Neither of them spoke again of the matter.

The next morning at eleven o'clock, Bronte said brusquely, "All right, it's comin' down. Head over to Pine Bluff and get that wire off. Be sure they know to have those cars over at Giddings in two days."

He stood there and watched as O'Dell left. He saddled his horse and flogged him out of sight down the road that was beginning to become striped with snow. Slowly Bronte pulled his cigar out of his pocket, lit it, and sent blue smoke spiraling in a gauzy haze into the air. "This time," he said, "we'll get rich."

★ ★ ★

"Lee, would you wait for a moment after the class is dismissed?"

Lee Morgan looked up quickly but saw on the face of the teacher no hint of what was wrong. He sat there while she dismissed the others, giving assignments, and when they were gone she got up and came down to his seat. He stood up at once and watched her warily. Ever since the fight between Reno and Lone Wolf, he had been sullen and uncommunicative. Reno noticed it, and Easy, and others, but there was little they could say.

"Lee," she said gently, "is anything wrong? You haven't been yourself for the past few days."

"Oh, nothin'," he muttered, refusing to meet her eyes.

Hesitating, she slowly reached out and put her hand on his shoulder. He looked up, startled, for she had never done such a thing before. When he saw that she really cared, he felt compelled to share his problem. "It's Jim and Lone Wolf. They had a fight. . . ." He briefly told the story and finished by saying, "I wish they hadn't done that. I—I don't know whose side to be on."

"You don't have to be on anybody's side, Lee. You can respect them both. You've been with Jim a long time, haven't you? And you like Lone Wolf, but you haven't known him very long."

"That don't matter," he said quickly. He was so tense and confused that he asked a question that he would never have asked under ordinary circumstances. "Miss Templeton? You don't hate Lone Wolf, do you?"

The question brought a flush to her cheeks, and she

knew that she must give nothing but an honest answer. Slowly she said, "When he first came here I did."

His lips drew into a thin line, and he nodded. "I thought you did, but I didn't know why."

"Nobody did, not even me, really," Sharon said. She could tell by his surprised look that a half-explanation would not do and she would have to tell him the story. "You see this scar, Lee?" She smiled faintly as he glanced at it, then dropped his eyes, unable to meet hers. "I got that in an Indian raid when I was a very young child. They wounded me, and they killed my father. Ever since then I've been afraid of Indians, and . . . and I've hated them, too. That was why when Lone Wolf first came I was unfair and unjust to him."

Lee was more confused than ever. He liked a simple world, as all boys do, where everything was black and white, every decision was yes or no. Now he was being pulled in two directions. And Sharon's confession complicated the matter still more. "Well," he said slowly, "I can see why you'd feel like that."

Sharon hesitated then said, "But I don't hate him anymore."

"You don't?" Lee's eyes brightened, and he said, "I bet it has something to do with the way he found you in the storm and saved your life, doesn't it?"

"Yes, it does. But, it wasn't only that." Sharon hesitated, then fixed her lips firmly and added, "While we were trapped in the cabin, I learned what a fine man he is. He did one thing that nobody has ever been able to do." She looked down at the floor, wondering if she could find the courage to speak. "You see, Lee, I've always felt that I was ugly because of this scar, and that no man would ever like me enough to marry me. But Lone Wolf . . . he made me see that that isn't so."

"Why sure it ain't," Lee cried eagerly, and he lifted his eyes and this time could look at the scar with the tolerance of youth. "It ain't so bad, especially when you keep your face turned." Then he flushed, knowing he had said a stupid thing.

Sharon laughed aloud. "It would be hard to go through life keeping your face turned from your husband, wouldn't it, Lee? But, anyway, I've learned something from Lone Wolf, and I'm grateful to him for it. But I don't want you to be frightened because this has happened between Jim and him. Men disagree and they fight, but they'll make it up, I'm sure."

"Do you really think so?"

"I'm sure of it. Jim is a good man, and so is Lone Wolf." She felt that she had done all she could, and she said, "You run along now, and I'll see you next week. It looks like this snow isn't going to stop. You'd better get home, or you'll get caught out like I was."

"Sure, I'll do that." He wanted to say he had to find Jim and somehow show him that he wasn't angry anymore and talk to him. Grabbing his hat and jamming it over his ears, he struggled into his coat and then left with a wave of his hand.

Sharon watched him go, then shut the door. She sat back down at her desk and noted that her hands were trembling. Despite her lightness of manner in front of Lee, she was distraught. She had been troubled ever since Lone Wolf had rescued her from the storm. For days she had gone over and over what he had said to her, everything that had taken place in that cabin.

She thought back over her life, how she had been bound by hatred against the Indians, how it had narrowed her life and controlled her emotions. To her surprise she began to weep. Helplessly she sat there, pressing her palms on the desk while the tears ran down her face, and then she gave in to the tears, lowered her head on her arms, and cried with great, racking sobs. Pain, grief, and fear stormed through her, and she wondered, *What's happening to me? Why am I so miserable and unhappy?* She had been cheered by Lone Wolf's words, and she had come to believe them in spite of the years of doubt and fear. But now her world seemed to be falling apart.

She forced herself to regain control of herself when she heard a horse pull up. She quickly reached for a handkerchief to wipe her tears away.

The door opened, and she saw Allen Danforth enter. "Hello, Miss Templeton," he said. "Thought I'd come and escort you home." He advanced through the aisle that separated the two rows of benches, and when he got five feet away he stopped abruptly. Sharon had tried to put a easy look on her face, but he saw her red, watery eyes and the tense strain in her expression. "What's the matter?" he asked.

"I—I don't know."

Danforth was a sensitive man, and he had given much thought to this woman. She had given him problems, and he knew that others had pressured her to be part of the movement to dismiss him, but that was not a problem for him. It was obvious that something had broken the will of this strong woman, and he wanted to help.

He moved around the desk, pulled up a chair, and sat there quietly, knowing that sooner or later she would either speak out or tell him to leave. The silence ran on throughout the room. It was so quiet that she could hear the faint cries of children playing far down the road.

She could bear it no more and said, "I don't know what's wrong with me. I'm so miserable."

"I'd like to hear about it if you think you can tell me," Danforth said quietly.

Sharon stared at him blankly, and an automatic refusal came to her lips. But she knew that she could no longer bury her feelings. Slowly she began to speak, and for thirty minutes she traced the history of her life. At times she would stop and struggle against the tears, and once when she spoke of the Indian raid, she broke down and wept again. Finally she got to the part where she had been in the cabin with Lone Wolf and related every incident of that. "There I was in an isolated cabin with a man that I hated," she whispered, shaking her head. "I told him what I told you about the raid. I told him about the scar and how I knew that it had forever taken away any chance of happiness."

When Sharon hesitated, Danforth asked, "What did he say?"

"He said that if a man loved a woman, this scar would make no difference."

"He was right about that. Others have been right about that, too, but you haven't been able to hear it. Sharon," he said, for the first time using her first name. "It took coming right up to face death before you were ready to listen."

His quiet answer drew Sharon's glance, and she studied him carefully. There was an emptiness and a weakness that seemed to flood her, and she whispered, "I don't know what it is. I've hated the Indians so long I think its soured everything in me."

"Hatred can do that." He hesitated and said, "There are no easy answers to these things, but there *is* an answer. May I tell you about it?"

She stared at him for a long time, then said quietly, "You mean religion, don't you?"

"No. I mean more than that. Everyone has a religion," he

said quietly. "But only in Jesus Christ is there the answer. He said that about himself. Did you know that? 'I am the way, the truth, and the life: no man cometh unto the Father, but by me.' He claimed to be the *only* way for men and women to find peace with God. The whole New Testament teaches that."

"I've seen some who had peace," Sharon said thoughtfully. "And I've seen a lot who have called themselves Christians who had nothing honorable about them."

"Of course you have. There have always been those who claimed to follow Jesus but were hypocrites or were simply misled. But you don't judge Jesus by those who fail him but by who *he* is. I think you're ready to hear about Jesus," he said. "May I read you just a small portion of the Scripture?"

Sharon hesitated then nodded. She sat back, and he pulled a worn Bible out of his pocket and opened it.

"In the fourth chapter of John, Jesus met a woman. It wasn't usual for men to speak to women in those days, especially not for Jews to speak to a Samaritan, which she was. But he came to a well, and a woman came to fill her pot with water, and he asked her for a drink. When she argued with him, he said, 'If thou knewest the gift of God, and who it is that saith to thee, Give me to drink; thou wouldest have asked of him, and he would have given thee living water. The woman saith unto him, Sir, thou hast nothing to draw with, and the well is deep: from whence then hast thou that living water? Art thou greater than our father Jacob, which gave us the well, and drank thereof himself, and his children, and his cattle? Jesus answered and said unto her, Whosoever drinketh of this water shall thirst again: but whosoever drinketh of the water that I shall give him shall never thirst; but the water that I shall give him shall be in him a well of water springing up into everlasting life.'"

He looked up from the Bible and said, "That's what it means to be a Christian. Do you understand that he was saying God has to be inside of you? That's the difference."

"I don't understand about the water," she said. "I never have."

"Look," he said carefully. "You've seen cisterns. You dig them in the ground or you make the container, and you fill it up with water, and what happens to that water? It gets moldy and stale, bitter and polluted, and it doesn't last. But what about a spring? It flows and flows and flows." He looked at her carefully and said, "Religion is like a cistern—there's no life in it. But Christianity is Jesus in your heart every day, flowing. So that when you speak or act or think, it's God, through Jesus Christ, flowing through you."

"I could never understand that."

"No, nor can I if you mean how it works. But I can tell you it does work. I've tasted the water."

For over an hour Allen Danforth read the Scripture, never pressuring, never raising his voice. There was a light in his eyes and compassion in his face such as Sharon had never seen before. Finally he read about how the Samaritan woman learned to trust in Jesus, and he said, "Finally, Jesus told her, 'God is a Spirit: and they that worship him must worship him in spirit and in truth. The woman saith unto him, I know that Messias cometh, which is called Christ: when he is come, he will tell us all things. Jesus saith unto her, I that speak unto thee am he.'" He closed the Bible and leaned forward and said, "Do you believe that Jesus is the Son of God?"

Sharon hesitated then nodded. "I've always believed that, ever since I was a child. I've just never been able to understand what it really means—or to do anything about it."

"Let me tell you how to do something about it, Sharon. It

is so simple that a fool will not err if he's honest with God."
Quickly he opened his Bible again, and he taught her the way
of salvation. He saw the Spirit of God begin to break her heart,
and her eyes filled with tears as he read Scripture after Scripture about the power of Jesus to save. Finally he said simply,
"Sharon, will you call upon God? That's all he asks you to do.
Turn from your sins, call upon God in the name of Jesus, and
he will be that spring of water in your heart."

He waited breathlessly, knowing this was the moment of
life or death, time and eternity for Sharon Templeton. His
heart gave a bound when she nodded her head and said, "Yes."

The two bowed their heads, and in a few moments she
began to pray, calling upon God. In an even shorter time she
began to weep, and Danforth knew that the work was done.
"You are now a child of God, Sharon," he said gently. "You can
believe that God is able to take you through all things." After a
time he said, "Let me walk you home."

She shook her head, saying, "No, I want to be alone for a
while, Allen." She put her hand out and her eyes were bright.
Her lips trembled as she said, "Thank you for coming by. I
know I'm different. The fear is gone for the first time—and the
hatred. Thank you for coming," she repeated.

Danforth saw her need to be alone and left. Sharon
walked around the classroom, thinking of all that had happened, and for a long time she could not bring herself to do
more than thank God for what he had done. Finally she pulled
on her coat, put her bonnet on, and started out the door. It was
a brisk walk of a few hundred yards to the house, and she
turned to go when she had heard a voice say, "Sharon?"

At once she turned and saw Lone Wolf, who advanced out
of the line of trees that banked the schoolhouse.

"Lone Wolf," she said in surprise and extended her hand. Surprised that he took it, she said, "I'm so glad to see you. Come inside so we can talk."

He followed her inside, and at once she took off her hat and coat and said, "I'm so glad you came. I talked to Lee, and he's so disturbed about the fight you had with Jim."

"That was wrong," Lone Wolf said, shaking his head angrily. "I was a fool. I've been wandering the hills ever since then." He shrugged and gave a bitter laugh. "Ashamed to go back. Ashamed to face my father or anybody else. Reno was right," he said. "I've been a worthless man."

"I'm glad you can admit it," Sharon said. She saw the surprise in his face, and she said, "I want to tell you something."

"What?"

"You remember in the cabin, how we talked? You probably don't remember all of it, but I've thought of every word. It's meant a great deal to me."

Surprise showed in his eyes, and he said, "What do you mean?"

She took a deep breath and said, "You told me that a man could love me, even though I'm scarred. I never believed that."

"I don't see how you could make so much of a scar. Of course, as I said, women are different." He held her eyes, and some of the tension left him. He smiled gently and said, "You have a beautiful face—and you have a beautiful spirit. I've always known that, in spite of your hatred. I could see beyond the hate. You have a good spirit."

Sharon shook her head. "No, I've been bitter, but I'm going to be different from now on." She hesitated then said, "I'm going to trust God with my whole life, and that means I will have no hatred." She put out her hand and said, "Forgive me for the way I treated you when you first came?"

Lone Wolf took her hand and held it. It was soft but strong. He could smell her perfume, and she made a lovely shape as she stood before him. The silence ran on, and he nodded and intended to say, "Of course I forgive you." And then, without meaning to and without planning it, he reached out, put his arms around her, and bent his head and kissed her.

The softness of her lips sent a riot of emotion racing through him. He was, of course, physically attracted to her. But beyond that there was a gentleness and a softness there that he had never found in other women.

Sharon had seen his intent but made no attempt to pull away. She was shocked herself at the kiss, amazed at how quickly things can change between people. He released her from his embrace, and she smiled at him, her lips tremulous. She did not speak for a while, then she said, "You're the first man who ever kissed me."

Her confession ran through him, and he could find no answer. "I'm leaving," he said finally. "I can't stay here any longer."

"Oh no. You can't do that," she said. And then she flushed. "I didn't mean to tell you what to do, but—"

"I don't know what I'd stay for," he said moodily. The touch of her lips had unsettled him. He stood there, a tall shape, his bronze face sculptured, looking almost savage with the braid, and then he looked at her with a strange expression. "I've said that no man would refuse you because of the scar. What about you? You're a woman, attractive. Would you refuse me because of what I am?"

Sharon blinked in surprise. She was an honest young

woman and spoke her heart without thinking. "No. I would not," she said. "You're a man that I've learned to admire and respect."

Lone Wolf lifted his head, stared at her carefully, then nodded. "I have to see Lee. After that I can come back, and we can talk some more."

"Of course, go to him—then please, come back."

She watched as he got on his horse and rode away into the growing darkness.

Lee had taken the long route home, going into the broken country of the east. He was running a small trap line there, and before he had gotten far, he was aware that he had made a bad decision. The snow was falling harder, and he turned left to take the pass that headed through Iron Mountain. He came unexpectedly upon a moving herd of cattle and stopped his horse. They were not moving alone, he saw, but two men were driving them. They were, he knew, part of Sun Ranch's herd, and at first he thought it was Jim or Easy. He galloped forward, calling out, "Hey, Jim! Easy!"

The figure on the horse closest to him turned at once. He was a burly man with a heavy beard, and he pulled his gun and aimed it at Lee.

Lee pulled his horse up abruptly, but there was no chance to move. "Hey, Con," the burly man said. "We got a witness here."

The other man left his small bunch of cattle, came over, and said, "You can either kill him, or we'll take him with us and let him go after we make the gather."

Lee's life hung in the balance. He saw the gleam in the

burly man's eye as he thought about killing him. But then he called, "Come here, kid." He moved his horse forward, and the rider pulled his rifle from his boot and said, "Put your hands out. I'm gonna tie you up, if you want to live, that is."

Lee nodded mutely, and quickly he was trussed into the saddle, his feet tied to the stirrups, his hands tied behind his back.

"You come along with us. We'll take a nice ride for a couple of days, then we'll turn you loose."

Lee had no choice but to agree. As the two riders herded the cattle along, he knew that there was no escape.

FOURTEEN
The Pursuit

Reno shrugged his shoulders in a worried fashion. Easy noticed, and the small rider said, "You're worried about Lee, ain't you, Jim?"

"He should've been here before this," Reno answered shortly. He reached over and pulled his heavy coat off a peg on the bunkhouse wall. "I'm gonna ride into town. He may have stayed over with somebody to wait this snow out."

Easy shook his head doubtfully. "Don't sound like him. It ain't snowin' that hard yet." He walked to the window and looked out. "Just enough to make a mess, and looks like it's gonna keep up. 'Member what a mess we had last time? I hope it don't get that bad."

Reno shrugged his way into the coat, pulled his hat down, and left, saying, "You take care of things till I get back. Tell Lillian I won't be any longer than I have to." He left the bunkhouse, saddled his horse, and rode out at once. The snow had been falling, not hard but steady enough to build up two inches. He did some arithmetic in his mind about how deep it would be if it didn't stop and shook his head. "Gonna be bad, maybe as bad as last time."

Three hours later, he pulled into town and went at once to the general store. "You seen Lee today, Kyle?" he asked.

"Lee? No. He was in yesterday before school and bought some candy. But I ain't seen him since." The storekeeper narrowed his eyes. "He didn't come home?"

"No. I'm going down and ask Miss Templeton. Maybe he stayed with her because of the bad weather."

"I doubt it," Kyle said, and as Reno left the store he said, "If you need help, we can get a search party going, Jim."

"Thanks, Kyle. I'll let you know." As he mounted his horse again, he thought, *That's a study in human nature. Here he's done everything he can to get rid of the preacher, one of the finest men I ever saw, but he's ready to go out in a storm and hunt for a boy. I guess I'll never figure people out. You just can't tell if they're good or bad.* He rode through the slanting snow, pulled up in front of the Middleton house, dismounted, and tied his animal. Taking the steps two at a time, he reached the door and knocked loudly. It was opened at once by Sharon. Her eyes opened in surprise, and she said, "Why—Jim!"

"Have you seen Lee, Sharon?"

She saw the strain in his eyes and said, "No, he left school at the usual time. He didn't come home?"

"No." The bleak, monosyllablic echo was a reflection of Reno's concern. He stood there hesitating, not knowing exactly what to do. Finally he said, "His horse may have fallen. I'm going to track back over the Short Hills just in case."

Sharon lifted her hand to her breast and said with alarm, "You don't suppose he went to see about those traps of his, not in this weather?"

Reno exclaimed, "Maybe so. He takes that way home sometimes, and I came into town the other way. I'm going to see if I can run him down." A thought struck him, and he said, "I wish I had Lone Wolf with me. He couldn't track in snow, but he's got ears and eyes. But he's probably still angry about that fight we had." He shook his head sadly. "I made a fool out of myself there, Sharon. But I'll make it right with him."

He turned, uttered a brief farewell, then mounted and rode off down the road. Sharon closed the door, and when Mrs. Middleton came to ask who it was, she explained the problem.

"Oh, my! I hope the boy's not hurt or lost! There's some pretty wild country out that way."

Sharon bit her lip. She could not think of anything to do, and then she remembered what Jim had said about Lone Wolf. "Ann," she said, "I've got to go out to Slash A."

"In this weather? You might get lost like you did last time."

Sharon did not even answer. She dashed up the stairs, quickly donned her heavier clothes, and pulled on heavy socks, boots, then a heavy coat. Leaving the house despite Ann Middleton's protest, she went to the livery stable, where once again she had to argue with Lynn Fogelman. Finally she said shortly, "Just saddle the horse, Lynn. I've got to go, and that's all there is to it!"

She left the stable as soon as the horse was saddled and rode steadily out in the direction of Slash A. It was only a two-hour ride, and the snow fell in small flakes and finally almost ceased. She kept the horse at a fast pace and pulled in at Slash A with a sigh of relief. As she dismounted, her legs were stiff from the cold, her hands were numb even though she wore gloves, and she had trouble tying the mare.

As she went toward the house, the door opened and

Mona came out to greet her, concern in her eyes. "Sharon, what in the world—?"

"Where's Lone Wolf?" Sharon asked hastily. "I've got to talk with him."

"Come in. I think he's out at the bunkhouse. You look frozen stiff." Despite Sharon's protests, Mona pulled her in and said, "You go into the living room, and I'll go get Lone Wolf for you. You need to thaw out."

"All right. But hurry, please!"

She moved into the living room, where she found Simon sitting at a large desk writing. He looked up at her with surprise and rose stiffly, saying, "I heard someone, but I didn't know it was you, Miss Templeton." He looked at her carefully and asked, "Is there trouble?"

"Yes. Lee Morgan left town yesterday and never got back to Sun Ranch. Jim just came to tell me."

"That young fellow?" Simon Meade exclaimed. "I hope nothing's happened to him."

They talked for a few moments, and then the door slammed. Mona entered with Lone Wolf at her side. He gave Sharon one quick look and said, "What's wrong?"

"It's Lee. He left school yesterday and never got home." Sharon shook her head in despair and said, "Jim just came in. He told me he was going out to the hills to search for him, but they're pretty big." She put her eyes on him and said, "Lone Wolf, it would help if you'd go look for Lee."

Lone Wolf stared at her and said, "He wouldn't take my help." His voice was sharp, and he walked out of the room.

Sharon stared after him in amazement, and then Mona exclaimed, "I think he's humiliated at taking a whipping from Jim. That probably never happened to him before."

"I'll go talk to him," Simon said. He shook his head sadly. "I hate to see that in him. He's been making good progress. I understand he talked to you."

"Yes," Sharon said. "I thought so, too, but I don't understand this."

"Indians have a lot of pride, I think. Especially in their physical ability," Meade said. "Like I've heard about the Chinese when they, what they call, lose face, some of them even kill themselves when they get humiliated."

Sharon said at once, "I'll have to go talk to him." She had taken off her coat, but she grabbed it up again and put it on. Meade followed her stiffly to the door. "I'll get the crew together as quick as possible. If Reno sends back to town, or if you know how to get word to him, tell him they'll be at Sun Ranch as quick as I can get 'em there. They can form a search party."

Sharon smiled at him and put her hand out. "That's thoughtful of you, Mr. Meade."

"Not at all—not at all!" Meade protested. "Wish I could go myself."

Sharon turned and left the house, noticing that the snow was starting to fall again. She looked across the yard and saw Lone Wolf moving toward the bunkhouse. He turned and saw her and stood there defiantly. She ran across the snow and, without thinking, took his arm and said, "You've got to help find Lee."

There was a stony look on Lone Wolf's face, and he shook his head. "I will go look, but I will not go with Reno."

Sharon grabbed his arm even tighter and said, "I know you care for Lee, and you can help him better by joining Jim and the others who'll be looking."

"He made me look small."

"Is the way people look at you more important than what you are?" Sharon asked. She reached up and touched her scar and said, "For years all I thought of was how people looked at me, and now you've taught me that that's wrong, and I'll never forget it. It's changed my whole life."

He hesitated and dropped his eyes, saying, "Well, I'm glad I was some help."

"I was wrong," Sharon said softly, "about Indians." Then she took a deep breath and said, "And now you're wrong. Can't you see that?"

Lone Wolf's pride was a strong thing. It ran through him like a steel bar, and he would have died rather than lose it. His training as a Sioux told him that he could not bend his will to help an enemy, one that had beaten him into the ground and disgraced him in the sight of the others. It was a code that he had never once broken. But now as he stood there, the tiny flakes of snow stinging his face, he looked down at the face of Sharon and saw the compassion in her eyes, the pleading that molded her lips into a soft shape, and he found that the law that he had lived by would not operate in this case. Somehow it ceased to be important.

Sharon said no more, for she saw the battle going on in the tall man, and finally he nodded and her heart bounded. "I'll go to Reno," he said.

Without thought she reached up and hugged him. She held onto him and buried her face in his chest, the rough material of his jacket rubbing her teeth. Then, embarrassed, she drew back, saying, "Oh, I didn't mean to do that." Her cheeks reddened, and she smiled slightly. "I'm just so happy for you. Thank you for helping."

He was embarrassed by what his Indian friends would have considered his womanish behavior, but he said, "I guess I'll go all the way." He shook his head. "I can't be an Indian anymore, can I, Sharon?"

"You had fine friends and a fine family there. But you have a new life now," she said. And then the urgency of the situation came back to her, and she said, "Go quickly, *Jason.* Find him."

"I will try." He whirled from her and ran toward the corral, and she watched as he put a simple hackamore on the stallion, leaped onto its back, and rode out of the ranch, the hooves churning the snow into a miniature blizzard.

★ ★ ★

When Reno rode back into Sun Ranch, he took one look and figured something had happened. The yard was filled with horses, and he slowed Duke's pace, wondering if perhaps Lee had been found and brought back dead. The thought struck him painfully, and as he pulled up to the hitching rail, the bunkhouse door opened and men piled out, led by Easy. Out came Dave Holly; Mason Deevers, a rancher over in the western section and a friend of the Reynoldses; Luke Short, a tall man with green eyes and blond hair, a southerner with several children; Bo Conland and Harry Trail, who had small spreads over in the short hills. Easy said at once, "We got a search party here, Jim. You didn't find him?"

"No, but I found something else that might mean something."

Chris Reynolds had run out from the house, followed by Lillian. They ignored the snow and came to stand in front of the group. Chris said, "What is it, Jim?"

Reno's eyes were bleak, and he said, "I took the trail that Lee usually takes on the way home, and I didn't see a sign of him. His horse wasn't down."

"We'll go comb them hills," Bo Conland said. "There's enough of us to find him."

Dave Holly said, "We can get some more men from town. Maybe I ought to send somebody in."

"There's no time for that," Jim said. "And I'm not sure that Lee is lost."

"Not lost? What do you mean, Jim?" Lillian asked quickly. She shivered in the cold wind and pulled the shawl closer around her shoulders.

Reno looked around and said, "It stopped snowing, pretty much, up in those hills over in that big pastureland that borders your place, Holly, and yours, Luke." The two nodded. "I found a trail of cattle tracks comin' out of your place, and some of them, a bigger bunch, seemed to come from Slash A."

"My cattle?" Holly exclaimed. "You must be wrong, Jim."

Bo Conland said, "I'm not movin' any cattle. What's up, Jim?"

Reno said quickly, "I've been thinking about it all the way here. My thought is that these rustlers are gonna take advantage of the storm and make a big haul. I think they've spread out and they're taking the cattle we've got furthermost off from the home ranches."

Silence fell over the group, and then Harry Trail said, "One way to find out. We can go follow the tracks."

Jim said, "That may be hard. It started snowing on my way back. Those tracks are gonna be covered up pretty soon."

"Which way were they headed, Jim?"

"Towards Logan's Gap." He saw a look of recognition run

through the men and said, "That's right. That pass leads over to the railroad. They're tryin' to get a big bunch of our cattle together and drive 'em out while we wait inside for the storm to end. By the time we'd get out, half our herds would've been gone."

"We gotta stop 'em, Jim!" Chris exclaimed.

"But can we find their tracks in the snow?" someone asked.

"I can find them."

Reno looked around to see that Jason Meade, who had evidently been in the bunkhouse, had come out to stand over to his right. Reno's eyes narrowed in surprise, but then a smile touched his lips. "I guess you could find 'em if anybody could, Lone Wolf."

Jason Meade stood there. He had come earlier to the ranch, waiting for Reno to return. But first he had gone to the small ranches in the valley to tell them the story and have the ranchers gather for a search party. He had led them to Sun Ranch only an hour before. Now he looked at Reno and said, "Call me Jason." He saw Reno's smile and knew that Reno understood what the name meant to him and to how he would live. "I was wrong to fight you."

Reno knew what the admission, simple as it was, had cost the man. He walked over and put his hand out. "Both of us were fools." A grin broke out on his lips, and he slapped the tall man's shoulder. "Time for us to fight somebody else."

Jason let out a gusty breath of relief, then asked, "But what about Lee?"

"The way I figure it," Reno said swiftly, "Lee was on his way home, and he had to come across their paths. He's bound to have seen those rustlers. I think they took him with 'em."

"Then we will go get him," Jason said.

Reno said, "Let's go gather some grub. We may be gone longer than you think. Everybody wear their heaviest clothes. Make sure you all got guns. You may have to use them."

An hour later they were riding out, and when they got to the road that led up into the pocket, Jason threw up his hand and the party stopped. "Let me go on ahead from here." He glanced up into the hills on his left and said, "That's the pocket, isn't it?"

"That's right," Jim said, then he understood why Jason asked. "Let's all ride in there together. If Bronte and his men are still there, we'll know that they're not rustlin' cattle, not this time, anyway. If they're not—" He paused and then said, "We'll know what to do. Do you know where Spanish Peak is, Jason?"

"The sharp peak over by Little Fork River? Yes, I know it."

"You try to pick up their tracks. We'll circle around in the pocket and meet you there. If we don't show up, they've killed us all," Reno said, smiling weakly. "A poor joke. Try to find them, Jason." Then he turned his horse and said, "Come on, let's go to the pocket."

They rode rapidly through the snow, which was again falling heavily. Within the hour they approached the draw that led to the cabin where Bronte and his crew hung out. "We'll go in slow," Jim said cautiously. "Fan out, and if anybody opens up on us, take cover and take care of 'em."

They moved cautiously down the winding trail until the cabin was in view. Jim called out, "No smoke."

They moved in still closer, and finally when they were close enough, Holly galloped ahead, jumped off his horse, and went to the door. He kicked it open, looked inside, came out, and mounted his horse again, saying, "Nobody here."

"All right," Reno said in a hard tone, "let's go to Spanish Peak."

"I sure hope Jason's got them varmints spotted," Easy said. "I'm plumb worried about Lee."

Reno glanced at him and knew that the small rider sensed his own dark mood and doubt, and even fear. Nodding, he said, "If they've taken him, they didn't kill him when they found him. We'll have to think they're holding him and will turn him loose when they get to the railroad. Come on, let's find Jason."

They rode back, circling through the pastures, and as they passed the tip of Sun property, Jim saw faintly the tracks of a large herd. "They got those fifty head that we had pastured over on the north forty, Chris."

"We'll get 'em back," Chris said grimly. "And we'll maybe find some ropes to convince them not to steal other people's cattle."

Jim thought, *What a difference has come over this young man since his days in the city,* but he said only, "We have to catch 'em first." Then the group turned and moved forward.

They found Jason waiting for them when they got to Spanish Peak and could tell that he had found something.

"A big herd's been by. Trail's almost all covered now. But they were headed straight through that pass."

"We'll kill these horses if we have to," Harry Trail said. He was nearing sixty, a spare, sparse man with brown eyes, and should not have been on such an expedition. "Let's go get 'em."

Reno said, "Wait a minute, Harry." He looked over the group and said, "This is gonna be rough. Some of us may not come back. Bronte's got a rough bunch."

Luke Short gave him a hard look. "We didn't come out to talk, Jim, or to play marbles. I'm tired of being swallowed alive by these rustlers. It's time to get 'em!"

Reno saw the same spirit in the others and said, "All right." He moved out then, and the horses snorted in the cold air, their breath rising in gusty spirals. There was a silence in the group as they thought about what lay ahead at Logan's Gap.

FIFTEEN
Shoot-out at Logan's Gap

The snow had laid a glistening white garment over the dark earth. A sharp wind whistled from the north, flipping the horses' tails and causing the men to pull their hats down more firmly over their eyes, which felt as if they were iced over. The cold was like a band that constricted their lungs, and even with their bandanas covering their noses and mouths the riders fought for breath.

"There he is," Easy muttered, his lips numbed by the biting wind. "Just where he said he'd be."

Ollie Dell, who rode beside him, had lost his dapper look. Ordinarily the neatest of men, he was now as tired and trail weary as any of the others. His clothes clung to him with a soddenness that irritated him. Looking across at Easy, he said, "You think he'll be able to take us to those buzzards? Can't track over snow."

"Don't know about that. We'll soon find out."

Reno and Chris Reynolds, riding at the head of the small procession, had seen the solitary horseman, and at once Reno spurred forward, the others following. When he pulled his horse up to a halt, he nodded, saying, "What about it, Jason?"

The cold seemed to have no effect on Jason Meade, which Ollie and others in the posse seemed to take as a personal affront. He wore deerskin britches and a shirt, a jacket made from buffalo hide, and a pair of moccasins over bare feet. His bronze face was rugged, and there was a gleam in his eyes that neither Reno nor the others had seen before.

"That way," he said, pointing toward the gap. "About four or five hours ahead of us."

Jim Reno, whose eyes followed the direction of Jason's gesture, nodded. "That's Logan's Gap. They're taking 'em to the railroad site at Giddings. They've got a couple days of pushin' to do, and they can't move too quick with those cattle. If we ride hard, we should come up on them pretty soon."

A mutter arose among the men, and it was Dave Holly who asked shortly, "How do you know where they're at, Meade?"

Jason slipped from his horse, stepped quickly to one of several small mounds. Using his toe, he kicked the snow away to expose cattle droppings. "Fresh," he said. His eyes gleamed almost with humor as he saw the chagrined look on Dave Holly's face. He knew he had yet to win the respect of these men, but right now he didn't care. His thoughts as he had found the trail had been only on Lee, and now purpose hardened in him as he said, "They're probably camped now. If we tried to catch them tonight, we'd be worn out for a fight."

Reno stared at him, turned, then looked over the posse. He did some arithmetic in his mind. From Sun Ranch there was himself, Chris Reynolds, Easy, Ollie Dell, and Patch Meeks. Shifting his glance, he saw the three men from Slash A—Charlie Cole, the foreman, Lew Meade, of course, and Baldy Sims.

The other small group that hung together included the ranchers—Dave Holly, Luke Short, Bo Conlon, and Mason Deevers. He spoke his thought aloud, "Thirteen of us," he murmured. There was a serious, thoughtful look in his dark eyes. "I expect they got more than that. I figure I'd take at least twenty to make that kind of gather and hold a herd together in this weather, maybe more."

Ollie Dell blurted out, "What difference does it make? I say let's go after them!"

"Well, James? What're we gonna do?" Easy asked.

Reno felt the pressure of the group's eyes and knew that the decision was up to him. He was reminded of the war when scenes like this had been enacted many times, when life and death hung on a single decision, and he had learned to make the decision instantly. Now, however, this was not war, and the life of a boy was at stake. Reno realized that he didn't look upon Lee as just a friend, but as a son, and he didn't want to jeopardize Lee's life by making a rash decision. He knew that the men who held Lee were deadly and ferocious, that they would kill without a second thought, and that Lee was helpless in their hands.

The snow was falling in tiny, granular flakes no bigger than the heads of pins. It stung his face and his lips, and he stretched in the saddle, placing his hands on the horn as he thought. Finally he said, "They'll come out on the other side of the gap sometime tomorrow, I think. Is that right, Jason?"

Jason replied, "Yes, I think so. Probably sometime late in the afternoon."

Reno nodded abruptly. "We'll have to ride around them, make a circle, and lay an ambush for them on the other side of the gap."

"Why, that'd be hard to do, Jim!" Lew Meade shook his head abruptly. "You know these hills. It's hard enough to get a horse to climb 'em when the weather's good. They'd slip and slide all over creation if we tried to take these slopes in this kind of weather."

"That's right," Mason Deevers added. "And it's too far to go to the passes to the south. We'd better just take off after them, Jim."

"No," Reno said sternly. "They'd know we were coming, and the first thing they'd do would be either to kill Lee or use him as a hostage. If Lee's still alive, I intend to keep him that way."

Reno's words still hung in the air when Jason said, "There is a way. I know it." He saw that his words touched the pride of the other riders. All of them had been in this country longer than he. A number of them had ridden the hills and valleys, the draws, and the plateaus. But Jason had lived in these hills since arriving in the country. "There is a way," he confirmed, speaking to all of them. "It's not big enough for a wagon, but it's a cut six miles north of here."

At once Luke Short shook his head. "I've been all over this country, and I ain't never seen no cut."

The group murmured, and Jason stood there in the snow, holding his horse by the halter. He made no other reply, for he knew that it was out of his hands. His eyes turned toward Reno, who was regarding him thoughtfully, severely, it seemed. For Reno it was hard to put trust and faith in another. He wanted to trust his own knowledge, but he knew that it was not enough. "All right, Jason. Can you get us around over the mountains and through the mouth of the gap over by Little Fork River? That's the way I figure they'll come out."

Jason nodded. "It's hard, but we can do it." He hesitated, then looked at the other men. There was something in his face that caught their attention. His bronze features still marked him out as different, and the dark braid hanging down his back made him look alien. They all watched him, waiting. Finally he said, "I am new here. You're all more experienced and have lived here much longer." He made a depreciating gesture. "I've wasted my time here doing nothing but roaming these hills, and I swear to you, the gap is there."

Easy slapped his saddle horn abruptly. "That's good enough for me, Jason. Now get us there."

His words seemed to break the spell, and Jason leaped astride his horse, kicked its sides, and moved across the snow at a fast trot. Reno gave Easy a wink and turned in his path, the others following. They made a parade across the snowy surface.

The hooves of the horses crunched the crusty snow, and Lew pulled up at once to ride beside Jason. He waited until the other man turned and looked at him, and then he smiled. "I'm glad you're here, little brother," he said quietly so that the others could not hear. "I wouldn't be able to do this. Neither would any of the others."

The words made Jason's face flush, and he shook his head. "I've been—" He hesitated, shook his head, then looked back at his brother. "It's been hard, but I want to come home, Lew." Then, as if the words embarrassed him, he kicked his horse into a slow gallop. Lew followed, his heart full, knowing that he had found his brother again.

None of them ever forgot that ride. Jason led the way up the mountain slope, followed by Reno, and the others trailed behind them. Easy brought up the rear, and everyone wondered if they would ever make it. The trail that Jason Meade led them to was not difficult at first, but soon the trees began to close in, and Reno, who was in the second position, was swatted across the face by a low-hanging limb. He blinked his eyes in pain and had to grit his teeth to keep from crying out. The sky had cleared and the moon was bright, but he could see nothing but the form of Jason, who rode ahead of him.

At the back of the line, Easy chuckled as he heard Ollie cursing. "Watch your language, boy," he said. "The good Lord hears you. His eye is on the sparrow and on us cowboys."

Ollie grunted as his horse slipped on the frozen slope. "I don't think he knows where we're going, and if I get slapped in the face one more time with a limb—" At that very moment he was caught on the cheek with a limb that Luke Short had pushed aside and let return. It raked across the young man's cheek, and he felt warm blood flow down his jawline. Yanking out his handkerchief, he wiped at it, saying, "This is worse than fightin' a war!"

"Don't ever say that, Ollie. There ain't nothin' worse than a war." Easy thought back on his days at Antietam, Gettysburg, and Chickamauga, days he had not thought of for a long time, and he said, "Ollie, don't be askin' for trouble. It'll come soon enough in this life. 'A man's born to trouble, as the sparks fly upward,' that's what the Good Book says."

At the head of the line, Jason peered sharply, picking out the spots to lead the procession. It was more difficult because of the darkness, and though he had made the journey twice, it was easy to become disoriented. Finally the land began to rise, and the horses grunted with exertion. He reached an impasse, a huge outgrowth of rock that dead-ended the trail, and said,

"This way. We'll have to go around." He turned his horse to the left, remembering how he had found this pathway weeks ago, but now it was only a little wider than the width of a horse. The evergreens grew closely together, mostly small trees only head high but flanked by the larger furs.

For two hours he kept on, and then finally he drew up the middle of a glade. The moon shone down, and he waited while the men emerged from the trail. When they were all there, gathered in the half circle, he nodded. "It's easier from here on."

"We wanna be in place before dawn," Reno said. "Can we make it?"

"I don't know about the horses; we may have to go on foot."

At once a murmur of protest went around, and Reno grinned. "I don't reckon we can do that, not in these boots. Do the best you can, Jason."

They rested the horses and then continued the climb up the slope. It seemed to Reno and the others that they would never reach the top, but finally they did. Once again Jason waited until they were all drawn up to the crest. The moon shone down brightly, and he glanced at it, then nodded. "If it weren't for that moon, I could never have found it."

"You did fine, Jason," Lew said warmly. "It'll be easier going down, I guess."

Jason thought about that, then said, "We still have to take some detours, but it'll be easier on the horses. We better go now."

They moved forward, and the going was easier since the vegetation was not as thick on this side of the mountain. The moon highlighted the trees that broke the white snow, and finally, when all of them felt that they could not go another mile, Jason stopped and held up his hand. "There's the gap," he said, pointing.

Reno looked up at the sky and said, "Another hour, maybe, before daylight. We've got to get set."

"You're running the show, Jim," Lew Meade said.

Reno grinned at him and shook his head. "We've got to plan this carefully. If it wasn't for Lee, it wouldn't be so hard."

"How do we get him away?" Jason asked quickly.

"First thing we have to do is locate him. We've got a pretty good view of the gap from up here. So here's what we'll do. I'll space you men out, some on each side. We let 'em go through until we see Lee, then we'll make our move."

Easy said, "He's bound to be guarded by somebody."

"I expect so. That's the problem."

Easy grinned rashly. "If there's one of 'em, I'll knock him out of the saddle."

Chris Reynolds blinked with surprise. "You mean—just kill him?"

"It'll give 'em to understand we're serious," Easy explained.

"We can't do that," Chris protested.

"Why not? They'll kill the boy quick as a wink," Jason argued. He looked at Jim and said, "Let me go try to work my way in. Maybe I can get him loose."

Reno thought about it, then shook his head. "He'll likely be in the middle of the herd, and even if you got him, you couldn't get out. We'll have to wait and make our play as we see it. Come along. Jason, you know the country. We need to scatter out on both sides. You show us where we can be hidden and yet still get a clear bead on them as they come through the gap." Addressing the posse, Reno said, "Once you get in position, try to get some sleep. We'll wake you and let you know what the plan is later. We're gonna need some shut-eye to be our best."

Jason turned his horse, and as they rode along one side of the gap, he pointed out half a dozen spots that would be good for cover. They then moved across the width of the gap that opened into a large valley, and they spotted the others' positions until everyone was stationed.

Finally Jason was alone with Reno as they rode around. As they rode forward and looked into the gap itself, he said, "We'll have to decide what to do when they get here." When Reno didn't answer, he said, "Easy had the right idea. Whoever's got Lee, we kill them and make sure that they don't put a gun on him."

"Hate to do that." Reno did not look at his tall companion. Thoughts were running through his mind. This to him was not like the war. He would not have hesitated then for an instant, but that time had faded, and now he said, "If we do, let me do it, and I'll try to wing whoever's guarding him." He sensed Jason's disapproval and said, "I don't like to kill a man if there's any way out of it."

The two of them rode forward for half a mile, then pulled over to one side and waited. Dawn came, the sun turning the bright snow golden and red, and they decided to get some rest, each of them switching watch every two hours. Around four in the afternoon, they were both awake and numb with cold, and Jason said, "They're coming."

Reno heard nothing, but he trusted Jason's hearing. "All right. You get on the other side, I'll stay with the men over here. We'll let 'em all pass until Lee comes. I'll work down this side. If he's on this side of the gap, I'll knock his guard out of the saddle. If he's on your side, you do the same."

Jason hesitated. "You know there'll be bullets all over the place. Lee won't know what to do."

"I think he will. Lee's smart," Reno said with a nod. "We'll make for him at once as soon as the guard goes down. Go spread the word."

Jason nodded and moved away, and soon they were all positioned. Jason had gone to every man, warning them to hold their fire until they heard his shots; then they could cut down on the others.

The silence fell over the land, and soon Reno picked up the sound of the bawling of cattle. Twenty minutes later they emerged from the gap, just a few at first, but then the gap seemed to be filled with the blackness of forms. The sunlight caught them, and he saw the riders on each side and behind. "Get ready," he called out. "Hold your fire until you hear my shot."

Reno watched carefully, along with the others, as the first cattle came through. He noted the men who urged them along, calling at them and hustling with their horses. They were in a hurry to make the train, Reno knew.

Finally he saw Lee, and he lifted his rifle and threw a shell into the chamber. There were two men with the boy, one on each side. He could not make out their faces because the sun glared in his eyes. As they drew near, he knew he would have but one chance. He drew his bead on the first man, held his breath, aimed at his shoulder, and pulled the trigger. The crack of his rifle caught the rustlers unaware, and Reno's aim was true. The man tumbled off his horse onto the ground, hollering, "I'm hit! I've been shot!"

Reno chambered another shell but then held his fire. The other guard had alertly grabbed Lee's reins and was sheltered behind him. He turned and moved back into the middle of the milling herd, and instantly an enfilade of shots rang out. Reno leaped over the fallen tree he had been hiding behind and ran toward his horse. He mounted at once, noting that the cattle had begun to stampede. When he came back, he saw that two men had bracketed Lee and were moving steadily back, using the cattle as a shield. He saw that it was Bronte and Faye O'Dell, and he called out, "Bronte, turn the boy loose." As he lifted his rifle, Bronte and Faye O'Dell pulled their guns and aimed them at Lee.

"Let us go, and the boy'll be all right."

Reno hesitated and said, "All right. Pull out of here. You're free to go."

Instantly Bronte called back, "We're taking the boy with us. We'll kill him if you don't agree, Reno. You know we'll do it."

Jim Reno hesitated but then saw that there was no other way. He cried out, "Hold your fire. Let 'em through."

The fire settled down into a crackle, then stopped, and Bronte said, "Let's go." He grabbed the reins of Lee's horse. The boy's hands, Jim saw, were tied in back of him. Bronte said, "If you follow us or try to take him, we'll kill him. You know we'll do it, Reno!" And then the two men spurred away, dragging Lee's horse with them.

There was nothing to do but watch as the three disappeared into the distance. The men gathered and began to attend to the half a dozen rustlers that had fallen, but Jason came to Reno and said, "They'll kill him anyway, Jim, as soon as they think they're clear."

"I know it, but if we go after them, they'll kill him, too."

Jason said at once, "There's only one way. Someone will

have to get in and pick them off before they know what's happening." He looked at Reno and nodded. "I think I'm the only one who can do that."

Reno hated the thought, but he knew that Jason Meade was right. "All right, Jason," he said hoarsely. "Go bring him back, and God go with you."

Meade gave him an odd look and nodded. "God go with me." Then he turned his horse and moved away, not hurriedly, allowing the trio to get beyond sight.

For the next half hour Jim was busy seeing to the wounded rustlers. Miraculously, none of them had been killed, but four of them were seriously wounded. The rest had scattered. Most of them at the rear of the herd, hearing the gunfire, had fled.

After tending to the wounded, the men gathered, and it was Easy who said, "What about Lee, Jim? Are we going after them?"

Reno shook his head, a bleakness in his eyes. "They'd kill him the first time they saw us."

"What'll we do, then?" Chris asked. "We can't let 'em just take him."

"Lew, take these guys and round up the cattle that you can and work them on back home. As for Lee, someone has to get in after dark and steal him." Reno paused and then looked toward the north. "And only a Sioux can do a thing like that!"

SIXTEEN
Night Stalk

Lee choked back a cry as he was jerked abruptly off his horse.
His feet were so numb that his ankles doubled under him. He
fell sprawling onto the ground, his face plowing into the snow.
His hands were tied in back of him, and he had no feeling in
them, for the rope that had tied him was so tight that he had
lost circulation, and the numbing cold had done the rest. As he
struggled to right himself and stand up, he was struck by a
kick that caught him in the shoulders.

"Get up, kid. There's nothin' wrong with you." Faye
O'Dell stood over him, and in the gathering darkness his face
wore a cruel expression. "What's the matter? You can't take a
little cold weather?"

"Cut him loose," Bronte said. He was tying his horse to
a sapling in the midst of a small grove where they had
paused. "He can't get away, and somebody's gotta get some
firewood."

O'Dell shrugged, reached into his pocket, pulled out a
pocketknife, and opened it. Bending over, he sliced the rope
binding Lee's hands. He raised the knife quickly to Lee's

throat, a grin stretching his lips humorously. "I could slit your throat, you whelp," he said.

Bronte looked over. He knew O'Dell to be totally unpredictable, and he said quickly, "You can do that after we get out of here. That bunch is liable to try to circle around, and we need this kid until we're out of the country." He glanced at Lee and shrugged, saying, "Kid, get some firewood." Then he turned to pull his blanket roll off his horse.

Lee got to his feet, beating his hands together to restore some circulation. He had said nothing on the long ride, and when the action had exploded he was exhilarated, knowing that it had to be his friends coming to rescue him. His exhilaration had faded, however, as the two desperate men had escaped, dragging him along at a rapid pace. It was hard to keep his hopes up. Catching a look from O'Dell, who seemed ready to add a heavy hand to his talk, he moved away quickly. It was still light, although only a few feeble gleams allowed him to look around, and he finally found a fallen tree. His hands were so cold he could hardly feel them, but he managed to find several small limbs and drag or carry them over to a spot beneath a towering tree where the snow was only an inch or so deep.

Bronte moved over and started building a fire, saying, "Get some bigger wood, kid."

Lee moved away, back into the forest. He found himself thinking, *I could make a break for it. Maybe they wouldn't catch me.* But then he knew that they would. He was numbed after his long ride, and they would ride him down on horses. He thought bitterly, *They need me to get out of here.* He had no illusions about what would happen afterward, for he knew already that both men were cold-blooded killers. He fought the fear that rose up in him and suddenly remembered the times that he and Reno had talked about God and prayer. He realized right at that minute that he needed God but found himself unable to do much praying. He had listened to the talk but had put it off for another day, and now he thought it was too late.

The two men back beside the fire watched as the yellow flames flickered higher as the wood caught, and O'Dell said with a curse, "It all blew up in our faces. I'd like to go back and put a bullet right through Reno's head."

"So would I," Bronte said. "But it's not worth dying for, even if we got him." Now, looking over at O'Dell, he shrugged, saying, "Sometimes it's down, sometimes it's up. Now it's down with us, Faye, but we'll make it out of this all right."

"Some of the boys didn't," O'Dell muttered. "I saw Burle go down, and Paint, too. I don't know where the rest of them were. Some of them are dead meat for sure." Again his eyes flickered with anger, and he gritted his teeth. "I wish they all had one head and I could put one bullet through it." He looked up then and saw the boy dragging a log back and said, "We can't let that kid go. He'd lead 'em right to us."

Bronte shook his head, motioning to O'Dell to keep his voice down. "Shut up," he said. "You don't have to let the kid know everything."

Lee had heard O'Dell and knew that there was no hope unless he managed to break away. He said nothing but worked on the fire, until it blazed fiercely. Bronte and O'Dell got out of their bedrolls and produced some food, and soon the smell of scorched beef filled the air. Lee was hungry but would not have admitted it to save his life. He pulled the saddle off his horse, took the blanket, and wrapped himself up in it, sitting back from the fire. He listened to the two men, who spoke mutedly to one another about their plans, which seemed to be to go to Mexico.

They'll never take me there, he thought. *As soon as they get clear, they'll shoot me.* An owl flew overhead, uttering a lonely cry that reached down into his spirit. He ducked his head, bit his lips, and determined not to show any fear, no matter what happened to him.

Finally, after the two men had eaten, Bronte looked at the fragment of steak on the stick he had grilled it with and tossed it over to the boy without a word. Lee was tempted to ignore it, but if he got a chance to escape, he figured he would need the strength. He picked it up and devoured it completely, then watched as the other two men drank coffee, of which they offered him none.

Finally O'Dell said, "Why don't we just keep riding, Jack? It makes me nervous knowing we're not more than a few miles ahead of those fellows."

"Because the horses would play out. They're already beat after a long day. They've rested their horses. I don't think they'll come after us tonight, but they probably will in the morning." At that instant he heard the owl hoot again and shrugged his shoulders. "That's the lonesomest, most miserable sound I ever heard—an owl hootin' on a winter night." He looked up into the sky, in which the stars were sparkling. "Let's get some sleep. We'll pull out before dawn, and the horses will be fresh. We'll get to the railroad and be out of this country."

O'Dell asked, "What about the kid?"

"Tie him to a tree."

O'Dell grinned, got up, and said, "Move over to that tree, kid." Slowly Lee got up, moved to a tree perhaps six inches thick, and at O'Dell's command put his hands behind him. He felt the rope bite into his wrists again. He tried to expand them so that he could wiggle them, but O'Dell was too smart for that. He gave the rope an extra pull that cut into Lee's flesh, and circled around to the other side of the tree. "Don't go away," he said. Then, in a mocking gesture, he picked up the blanket and threw it over Lee. It stuck on his legs but left his torso completely uncovered. O'Dell laughed, went back to his bedroll, and stretched out in front of the fire. Bronte piled several large logs on the fire and looked over at Lee with an expressionless face. Without a word he, too, pulled his blankets around him and went to sleep.

Lee sat there, and the time wore on slowly. He had no watch, and the night crept by on leaden feet. His hands, once again tied, grew numb and lost all feeling. The cold bit into him, and he began to shiver. The two men had fallen asleep at once, and Lee knew that this was his last chance. *But there's nothing I can do,* he thought. He strained against the rope, knowing it was hopeless. He looked up, wondering if he could pull the tree over, but that was impossible as well. As he sat there he thought about his early life, the hardness of it all. And then he thought of Reno and how the cowboy had found him and taken him along. Reno had been everything to him: older brother, father, family. And then Lee prayed. It was simple enough. He said, "Oh, God, I'm not fit to pray. You know what I am, but if it ain't too much to ask, let me get out of this. Give me some more time. . . ."

His lips moved for a time and then shut firmly. The cold seemed to sap his strength. The only sound was the crackling of the fire and, once again, the cry of the night bird. And then he felt something touch his forearm. A start of fear ran through him and he jerked forward, but a hand reached around and clamped itself over his mouth so he could not speak. Then the hand loosened, and a form appeared beside him. "Jason," he whispered.

Jason glanced quickly at the two sleeping men and held his finger up to his lips. He smiled once at the boy then moved back, reaching for his knife, and Lee felt the rope suddenly go slack. His hands were free, and he tried to flex them. Lee sat there, knowing his legs were numb. He looked at Jason and pointed at them, and Jason nodded and began to rub them as Lee rubbed his hands. All the time Jason kept his eyes fixed on the two men.

Finally, Lee felt the blood coursing through his legs and nodded. Jason returned the nod and motioned for him to get up. Slowly, carefully, Lee moved his feet under him, and Jason grasped his arm and pulled him upright. Jason motioned toward the darkness, and Lee understood that he was to go into the woods where Jason, no doubt, had tied the horse. He nodded and moved as carefully as he could, but his ankles betrayed him. His feet were almost frozen. He stepped in a pothole, his ankle turned, and he fell headlong with a grunt.

Awakened, the captors threw their blankets back, and Lee, lying flat on his back, saw that they were pulling their guns. It was almost magical the way O'Dell had his gun free of the leather, and Lee knew that he and Jason were dead men.

But O'Dell hesitated, a cruel smile on his lips. This was something he enjoyed doing, and he wanted to make the moment last for a few more seconds. He said, "Well, Injun. You didn't do—"

His voice stopped abruptly. Lee did not see the throw, but he had seen so many times how Jason drew his knife from its sheath, threw it in a quick, snapping motion, and buried it some-times into a tree up to half the length of the blade. Now that same blade buried itself up to the hilt in the throat of Faye O'Dell! The gunman's fingers tightened on his gun, and an explosion ripped the air. O'Dell fell back, pawing at his throat. But there was no time to waste, for Bronte was drawing his own gun, scrambling to his feet. Lee was suddenly grasped in arms of steel, snatched up, and bounced onto Jason's shoulder as the big man whirled and ran into the thicket. Bronte's gun spoke three times, and with the third shot Lee felt Jason lurch and grunt. However, the pace faltered only for a moment, and Lee felt the branches claw his face as Jason plunged into the deeper woods. He could also hear the sound of Bronte pursuing.

Jason dropped Lee behind a tree and said, "Stay here. Be quiet." And then Jason was gone.

Bronte, having taken one quick look at O'Dell and seeing that his companion was dead, had fired his shots and was rea-sonably sure he had winged the big man. "Can't let them live," he grunted. "I've got to stop their clocks!" He picked up O'Dell's revolver, ignoring the crimson stream that ran down the white throat onto the ground, and plunged into the forest. The stars were bright and the moon was up, and he knew that the two could not be far away. *He'll never leave the boy. He's got to be here someplace!* He plunged on, the branches raking across his face. He pulled his hat down and bulled his way through. He kept glancing from side to side, just for a glimpse, and finally stopped, sucking for breath after the sudden exer-tion. *He's got to be here,* he thought wildly. Slowly he began to backtrack, stopping every few moments to listen. Once he stopped for at least two minutes, standing absolutely still, and heard nothing. His heart was pounding. There was something

frightening about the silence. He *knew* that the man he had
shot was somewhere—but *where?* He began his progress
through the woods, and as he passed beside a large fir tree,
his feet making loud crunching noises in the snow, something
struck his right wrist. He let out a cry as the revolver dropped,
and he turned, his other gun in his left hand. But this time a
fist caught him directly in the mouth and drove him backwards. Instinctively he pointed the gun and pulled the trigger
again and again, until he had fired four shots. He kept from firing the last two, and as he scrambled to his feet he looked
across the snow that was glistening under the moonlight.

Nothing!

No one was there, and there was no sound. His hands
were trembling now, for he had not heard a sound before he
was attacked. He knew Indians could stalk silently, and now he
knew that was true even over snow that crunched beneath his
own feet. He was gripped by a fear that was like nothing he
had ever known. The night was silent, the snow appeared
ghostly white in the moonlight—and somewhere death
roamed looking for him. Without intent, he broke into a run,
heading for the clearing, but he had taken no more than five
steps before a voice cried out, "Stop where you are, Bronte."

With a cry, he whirled and, seeing Jason step from
behind a tree, lifted his revolver and fired. The shot missed,
and at once Jason lifted his gun and returned the shot. As the
slug caught Bronte in the side and turned him sideways, his
finger tightened on the trigger, sending the last bullet harm-
lessly into the air. He fell to the ground, grabbing his side, pain
running through him. He looked up wildly to see that Jason
had come to stand over him. His mouth went dry as Jason
Meade slowly pointed the gun directly into his face. The pain

was running through him, but Bronte gasped, "Don't—don't kill me." His voice became hysterical, and he cried, "You can't shoot a wounded man!"

The hand holding the gun was steady as a rock. The barrel did not waver, and those blue eyes so strangely illuminated in the dark face of Jason Meade were like gimlets. They seemed to glitter like the eyes of a wolf closing in on his prey.

And then, as Bronte gave it up, knowing that he was a dead man, Jason lowered the gun and said in a voice filled with wonder, "No, I guess you're right. I can't kill a wounded man." Then he smiled and slipped the gun into his belt. "All right, Lee. You can come out now."

Lee appeared almost at once, his face pale. He had heard the gunfire, and he gave a sigh of relief as he came to stand beside the big man. "You're all right? You got him!"

Jason saw the light of admiration in Lee's eyes and said, "I guess I'm not an Indian anymore, am I, Lee? An Indian would've killed him where he lay."

Lee looked down at the wounded Bronte, who was clutching his side and gasping for breath. Then he looked back at Jason and said, "I'm glad you didn't kill him, Jason." He hesitated then said, "I'll-I'll bet Miss Sharon'll be glad, too."

Jason's eyes brightened for a moment, and then he shook his head. "I don't know, maybe so." Then he shut his eyes and began to sway like a tall tree.

Lee remembered that Jason had been shot. "Jason," he said, "where did it get you?"

"In the back." He saw the alarm on Lee's face and said, "We'd better stop the bleeding if we can."

He pointed the gun at Bronte and motioned toward the

fire. Bronte stood, holding his side. Bronte's wound, though serious, was not fatal. When they got to the fire, Lee quickly, frantically, found and ripped a shirt that Bronte had been carrying in his saddlebags, wadded it up, and lifted Jason's shirt. The wound, he saw, was high up, and his heart sank when he saw the scarlet blood flowing. But Jason said, "I think it hit me at an angle. I'd be dead if it hit me square on. Tie it up tight as you can, Lee."

Lee made a compress by folding the cloth over. He pressed it against the flowing blood and tied it as tightly as he could, winding the bandage around Jason's chest and over his shoulder. "That's not gonna stop the bleeding," he said, shaking his head. "We've got to get you back to a doctor."

"What about me?" Bronte demanded. "I'm bleedin' to death."

Jason gave him a hard look and gestured toward the saddlebag. "Be your own doctor," he said. "And hurry up about it. We've got a long way to go."

Bronte cursed and staggered to his horse but made himself a bandage of sorts from another of the shirts in his saddlebag, and then Jason ordered him to get on his horse. When he was on, Jason said, "Lee, tie his hands to the saddle horn, and tie him tight." When Lee had done this, he said, "Now tie his feet underneath that horse's belly." When Lee had accomplished this, he said, "Now put a rope around his neck, and keep it on your own saddle horn."

As soon as they were ready, Jason walked over to O'Dell's body and looked at him, shaking his head. He then withdrew the knife from the man's neck and wiped it in the snow. "Let's go," he said, struggling onto his horse. He led out and Lee followed. Bronte, fearful that he might fall off his horse and be strangled, rode as close as he could. Lee kept a close eye on him but an even closer eye on Jason. He knew that the make-shift bandage would not stop the blood.

Jason said nothing but rode on. They had gone five miles when he felt himself reeling in the saddle. He reined in his horse and held onto the horn, gripping with all his might. He felt himself slipping, and then he hit the snow, lights blinking before his eyes. Lee was off his horse in a flash and tied it to a sapling. He pulled O'Dell's gun and aimed it at Bronte. "If you move," he said, "I'll blow you out of the saddle." Then he bent over and saw that Jason's eyes were fluttering. "Are you all right, Jason?" he said.

"Not too good." Lee rolled him over and saw that the bandage was blood soaked. He did not know what to do and stood there, trying to think. He could not get the big man back into the saddle, he had to be watchful of Bronte, and he felt so alone. He remembered his prayer the night before and prayed again: *God, you've got me out of this, now get Jason out of it—please!*

Not more than five minutes later Lee, who had wrapped a blanket around Jason and was trying to think, heard a voice and looked up to see a horseman coming out of the timber. Thinking at first it might be one of the rustlers, he lifted his gun, and then a familiar voice cried out, "Lee! Lee! Are you all right?"

"Jim!" Lee almost dropped the gun but stood there filled with joy as he saw Reno ride in.

Reno swung off the saddle and came to Lee at once, his eyes running over the youthful expression of the boy, then he gave him a surprising hug. His voice was husky as he said, "I'm glad to see you, Lee."

Lee felt warm over the hug, but he said, "Jim, Jason's shot. We've gotta get him to a doctor."

Reno whirled, his eyes taking in Bronte and the bloody shirt bound to his side. He said, "Lee, watch him." Then he turned to Jason. Bending over, he pulled the bandage back, examined the wound, and shook his head.

Jason had been vaguely aware of all this, and he opened his eyes and saw Reno. Then he looked over and saw Bronte glowering at him. His eyes came back to Reno, and he said sleepily, "I guess I'm not an Indian anymore, Jim. I could've killed him, but I didn't. No self-respecting Indian would 've done a thing like that."

Then a cold wave of darkness seemed to wash over him, filtering over his eyes and silencing every sound, and he dropped into a deep, black, bottomless hole.

SEVENTEEN
The Beginning of Something

The layers of darkness that had covered him began to dissolve. Faint rays of light slanted down, piercing the murky gloom that had encased him. He turned his head to one side, and as he did, he felt a hand on his forehead and a soft voice said, "Jason—Jason, are you awake?"

Turning his head back, he opened his eyes, blinking against the golden sunlight that flooded through the windows. A woman's face was framed by the light, which created a halo around her hair. "Sharon . . . ," he whispered, and he was shocked to find when he tried to lift his hand that it was a labor.

Sharon took his hand and held it for a moment, and there was a breathiness in her voice as she said, "Thank God you're all right!" She held his hand tightly and waited for him to speak.

Memory flooded back to his mind, and he licked his lips and said, "Can I have a drink of water?"

"Yes, of course." Getting up in a swift motion, she moved to the washstand, poured water into a glass, came back, and helped him struggle into a sitting position. She put the glass to his lips, and he drank thirstily, then lay back against the pillow. "How long have I been here?"

"Two days," she said. The doctor was here and took the bullet out. He says you were lucky. Then she shook her head and her lips grew firm. "No, not luck. It was the Lord looking out for you."

He gazed at her thoughtfully, his mind still not completely clear. "You believe that, don't you? That things turn out all right."

"Yes. I don't know why, not after what I've been through, but now I do."

He knew she referred to the scar on her face. He reached up with his left hand and touched it gently, saying nothing. She sat very still, not moving as his fingers traced the ragged scar. Finally he lowered his hand and said, "I'm glad you think that. I hope you always do."

She reached out and pushed his hair back off his forehead. "You're going to be all right," she said gently. "I want you to talk to your father."

Jason hesitated then nodded. "Yes. I must do that. Before you go get him, let me tell you this." He hesitated, then put his hand out, which she took. He held it for a moment, marveling at the softness of her skin, then said quietly, "I love you, Sharon. I don't know where I'm going or how I'll get there. I've got a lot of changing to do, but I hope—I hope you'll be there for me."

Tears stung Sharon's eyes. She leaned over quickly, laid her lips against his, and held them there for a brief moment. Then she pulled back, saying, "My dear, of course I will! I'll always be here!" She left the room at once, dashing the tears from her eyes, and went to where Simon Meade sat in a chair, looking out the window. He got up as she entered and demanded at once, "How is he?"

"He wants to see you," Sharon said. She saw the doubt in his eyes, and she went to him and touched his arm. "He's changed, Mr. Meade. He's not the same. I can tell."

Meade stared at her carefully. He had not been a wise man in all things, but he was experienced enough to sense something of what was happening. "I suppose," he said off-handedly, something like a smile tugging at his lips, "I'll be seeing quite a lot of you, Sharon. Won't I?"

Her cheeks were tinged suddenly with a pink color, and she dropped her head in embarrassment. He reached out, lifted her chin, and said, "I can think of nothing I'd like better. We'll talk of this later."

He moved across the room, limping, but with a strong determination etched in his features. When he got to the door to the room where his son lay, he stood there one moment, afraid to go in. There had been so much that had happened, so much pain. His life had been full of bitterness, and now that had changed. He bowed his head thoughtfully, and for the first time in the many years since his wife had died, he said under his breath, "Thank you, God, for restoring my son!" And then Simon Meade opened the door and went in to greet Jason.

Mona looked up and said with surprise, "Look, Lew."

Lew looked out the window and saw a buggy coming. "Why, it's Lillian," he said. "Who's that with her?" He stood up, looked closer, and said, "It's Lige." He turned to face her, a peculiar expression on his face. "Guess they came for a visit."

They waited till the footfalls on the porch announced the visitors, and Lew went at once to the door, saying, "Come in, you two." Lige and Lillian entered, and Lige had a strange expression on his face. Lillian also seemed nervous as they greeted one another and made small talk. Finally Lillian said, "Mona, I know you may think this strange—" Then she could say no more. She bit her lip and stared at Mona with something like a pleading in her eyes. There was a pride in this woman that ran very strong, but something, her daughter understood, had changed her deeply. And then suddenly Mona understood.

Looking at Lige, who smiled at her and nodded, Mona went at once to her mother and threw her arms around her. "I can think of nothing better, Mother."

Lew stepped forward and shook Lige's hand, saying, "Why, you sly devil. Courting my mother-in-law behind my back."

All four of them laughed at that, and finally Lillian shook her head. "I didn't know how you'd take it. It was hard to tell Chris. You both know how I loved your father, but—" she looked up at Lige—"it's been lonely, especially now that you're gone, and one day Chris will be gone."

Mona nodded, a smile illuminating her face. "You'll be very happy, and I intend on planning the wedding. We're going to plan that wedding, aren't we, Lew?"

"That's right. We'll spare no expense."

The four of them stood talking and laughing, and finally, Lillian motioned her daughter off to one side and whispered, "I'm as nervous as a woman ever was, even at my age."

"Mother, you're beautiful, and you're going to have such a good life with Lige. The two of you are made for each other." She looked over to where the two men were talking and said thoughtfully, "When Jim Reno brought us out to this place, I doubt he knew he'd be running a matrimonial bureau."

"It was Jim, wasn't it?" Lillian realized. "I'll never cease to be grateful for him. He's become like one of the family. I can't wait to tell him." However, when Lillian went back to Sun Ranch, she discovered that Jim Reno was not at all surprised. She told him rather bashfully of how she was going to marry the sheriff and that Lige was going to come and live on the ranch, giving up his badge. Reno grinned at her crookedly. His black hair shone in the sunlight as they sat on the front porch, where she'd called him, and the lines of his face were clean and smooth. "Why don't you tell me something I don't know, Lillian?" he said. "You look like a bride. A man has to be blind not to have seen what was happening to you. Lige will make a good man for the ranch."

"We owe it all to you, Jim," Lillian said. "We'll never forget it. Never. If you hadn't come for us and brought us out here, why, I don't know what would have happened to us." She leaned forward and touched his hand and said, "I thank God for you. I know he used you to save us all as a family."

Reno considered that, his eyes thoughtful. "I hope you're right. I've done so many things I'm not proud of, I'd like to remember this one as something in my credit."

"We'll have a long time to talk about it," Lillian said.

Everyone agreed that the wedding of Lillian Reynolds and Lige Benoit was picture-perfect. It had been held at the Sun Ranch, and the house had been too small to hold the guests. Nevertheless, they had crowded in on the porch and looked in the windows while the two were made one by Pastor Danforth.

Jason was there, standing beside his father. Gone was the braid, and he was wearing a black suit, looking no different from the elder rancher except taller and more bronzed by the weather. After the wedding was over and the bride had been thoroughly kissed, Jason looked across at Sharon, and a smile touched his lips. Then he asked, "How many horses did you have to give for her, Lige?"

A laugh went up, and Reno could see that the tall young Meade was finally accepted. He squeezed Lee's shoulder, and when the boy turned, he winked at him and whispered, "It's gonna be all right, Lee. It's gonna be all right."

Two weeks after the wedding, Lee and Easy were sitting on the corral fence watching Reno as he fought a wildly bucking bay stallion to a standstill. He had been thrown several times, so he was covered with dust from head to foot, and there was a grimness in his jaw. He gripped the reins, trying to pull the horse's head up, and waved his hat with his other hand. As the horse went down he raked it across the shoulder with his spurs, but despite all he did, the mighty horse made a crow hop and twisted like a corkscrew, sending Reno flying like he was shot from a catapult. He hit the ground and rolled over, and when he sat up, there was blood on his lips. Slowly he got up and stared at the horse intently. Both Lee and Easy expected him to go back and mount again. Instead he picked up his hat, knocked the dust off of it, settled it on his head, and then walked over to where the two men sat.

"You know," Easy said, "I always heard there never was a horse that couldn't be rode and never was a rider couldn't be throwed."

Reno managed a grin. "Well, I can testify to that last. I thought I was a pretty fair rider, but that horse has thrown me seven times." He looked over and stared defiantly at the bronc, who was watching him with a wild eye. "That is sufficient," he said with finality in his voice. "Let somebody else get his neck broke!"

The dinner bell rang, and Easy slid off the corral fence. "Let's go chow down. My stomach thinks my throat's been cut."

Jim and Easy turned to go, but Reno said, "Wait a minute." They turned back to him, and he tilted his hat back on his head. The sun was going down, and he seemed to be admiring the rosy touch that it gave the mountains over to the east. They were accustomed to his pauses in speech, and Lee as well as Easy knew he was winding up to tell them something.

Lee shifted his feet up comfortably and finally said, "What is it, Jim?"

Reno's eyes turned to meet the boy's, and he said, "Well, with Bronte in jail, I guess our job here is about done, Lee. We'll be leaving."

"Leaving?" Lee asked in dismay. He had learned to love the place and looked forward to learning more of the Indian skills from Jason Meade. "Where are we going?"

"I don't know," Reno said. A thought came to him, and he said, "I think, Lee, you better stick around here. Lillian will be glad to have you. I know how much you admire Lige. Me, I'm just a fiddle-footed scoundrel."

Lee bit his lip, and frustration made lines on his youthful face. He looked down at the ground, and Reno continued to speak of the advantages of staying on at Sun Ranch. In truth, he felt guilty about not providing more for the boy, and he had practiced this speech. It was hard for him to make, but now he said, "Be better all around. You stay here and learn the ranching business."

Lee looked up, pain on his face. "You don't want me, Jim?"

Reno blinked his eyes. "Want you? Why, I never said anything about that. But it'd be better for you." Easy saw the boy shake his head stubbornly, and he knew what to do. "Why, you wouldn't last two weeks without Lee and me to take care of you, James Reno." He slapped Lee on the shoulder and said, "We've got to go along and see that this fellow doesn't go plumb downhill. Come on, let's do some figuring. Which way you think we ought to go, Lee?"

Lee shrugged his shoulders and said, "I don't know."

Easy said, "Let's go eat while I'm thinkin'. I always think better when I got a full stomach." He winked at Reno, and the three moved toward the house. "Now I've always heard that you could dig a hole and end up on the other side of the world in China. Do you reckon," he asked, "that them Chinese would be standing on their heads when we got to 'em?"

Reno smiled but halted as he saw Lige and the mayor of Banning ride in. As they pulled up in front of Reno, Reno greeted them.

"You look like you've been on the wrong end of a whippin'," Lige commented.

"That's about the size of it," Reno agreed. "That new stallion saw to it that no one rode him again today."

"Well, Reno," the mayor said, "perhaps I can help you out with your problem."

"What problem is that, sir?"

"Why, the problem with trying to tame a mean-spirited horse!" The mayor chuckled, then continued. "Seriously, Reno, Lige and I have been talking about Banning's need of a new sheriff now that he's taking up the quiet life of a rancher. And we both agree—as does the town council—that you'd be perfect for the job."

Reno was silent as he thought about what the mayor had said. *I was thinking it would be good for Lee to settle in one place, and this way we could still be together. But, then again, I've already been here longer than anywhere else recently.*

He looked over at Easy and Lee. "What do you fellows think?"

"Whal, James," Easy started, "it seems that you've been takin' care of these desperadoes around here already. Why not get paid for it?"

Lee's eyes were bright as he said excitedly, "Then we could be together, and I could still go to school and learn about nature from Jason. It'd be great!"

"And you know that Lillian would love to have you near to us after all you've done for her and the kids," Lige added, hoping to make it impossible for Reno to say no.

Reno looked at their faces and knew what everyone else wanted. Now he looked inside himself to see if he wanted the same. After a few moments, he said, "Mr. Mayor, I've never been one to stay in one place for more than a few months at a time. My kind just seems best at drifting around, never getting anchored to any one place." He saw the disappointment form on the mayor's face, but he continued. "You're town has been great, and the people around this area are some of the finest. And it seems obvious that a lot of people want to keep me around." Reno paused before giving his answer, not sure what the answer would really be. Finally he said, "This town and these ranchers have made me a part of the community, and I guess I owe it to them to do the job they'd like me to do. I'd be honored to be Banning's sheriff."

Easy and Lee yelped with joy. Lige and the mayor smiled and shook Reno's hand, assuring him that he had made the right decision.

Reno stepped over to Lee and Easy and put his arms around his friends. "It looks like we finally found a place to settle down. I couldn't have picked anywhere better! Let's go get some grub and celebrate."

Gilbert Morris is the author of many best-selling books, including the popular House of Winslow series, the Reno Western Saga, and The Wakefield Dynasty.

He spent ten years as a pastor before becoming professor of English at Ouachita Baptist University in Arkansas and earning a Ph.D. at the University of Arkansas. Morris has had more than twenty-five scholarly articles and two hundred poems published. Currently he is writing full-time.

His family includes three grown children, and he and his wife, Johnnie, live in Orange Beach, Alabama.

In addition to this series . . .

RENO WESTERN SAGA
#1 Reno   0-8423-1058-4
#2 Rimrock   0-8423-1059-2
#3 Ride the Wild River   0-8423-5795-5
#4 Boomtown   0-8423-7789-1
#5 Valley Justice   0-8423-7756-5

. . . look for these captivating historical fiction titles from Gilbert Morris . . .

THE WAKEFIELD DYNASTY
This sweeping saga follows the lives of two English families from the time of Henry VIII through four centuries of English history.
#1 The Sword of Truth   0-8423-6228-2
#2 The Winds of God   0-8423-7953-3
#3 The Shield of Honor   0-8423-5930-3

THE APPOMATTOX SAGA
Intriguing, realistic stories capture the emotional and spiritual strife of the tragic Civil War era.
#1 A Covenant of Love   0-8423-5497-2
#2 Gate of His Enemies   0-8423-1069-X
#3 Where Honor Dwells   0-8423-6799-X
#4 Land of the Shadow   0-8423-5742-4
#5 Out of the Whirlwind   0-8423-1658-2
#6 The Shadow of His Wings   0-8423-5987-7
#7 Wall of Fire   0-8423-8126-0
#8 Stars in Their Courses   0-8423-1674-4 *(New! Fall 1995)*